Excelsior

Seeking the Beyond

GEORGE ALSTON

Matador
Unit E2 Airfield Business Park,
Harrison Road, Market Harborough,
Leicestershire. LE16 7UL
Tel: 0116 2792299
Email: books@troubador.co.uk
Web: www.troubador.co.uk/matador
Twitter: @matadorbooks

ISBN 978 1805140 429

British Library Cataloguing in Publication Data.
A catalogue record for this book is available from the British Library.

Printed and bound in Great Britain by 4edge Limited
Typeset in 11pt Minion Pro by Troubador Publishing Ltd, Leicester, UK

Matador is an imprint of Troubador Publishing Ltd

Ever higher, ever onward.

A Strange Way

1

Simone Carrier followed the sneaky train for thousands of feet. It trundled its passengers like sheep to their chosen destination. Then she changed tack and moved, from wingtip to wingtip, followed by a westward flight towards the chosen mountains of Chamonix, nestling in the cool air beyond. She was light and intrepid – her nylon top flew like a bird. She was as fast as the parapente which would take her, risking her life pushing and pulling – yet, faster than any man she knew – in France!

Steve Carson was one of the unfortunate people on the overnight train from Paris. It pulled into Le Fayet at breakfast time. The morning sunshine sparkled on the carriage windows and reflected a panorama of Alpine meadows and snowy peaks. No matter how many times Steve Carson had been to the Alps, when he next saw them, they always stirred something deep inside his spirit.

He stood on the steps of the compartment, swept back his long dark hair and mouthed a silent 'Wow!' to the gods. 'Those whom they love they take,' he whispered. It would be a good place to climb the highest mountains and in which to live and to die.

Simone Carrier said the same thing. She lived life on a budget. She could swing a kite around and pull it up in a matter of seconds – avoiding a crash landing. Steve Carson could do the same thing with his ice axe – fall and be held by the axe, in a fraction of seconds. It was a question of whether they wanted to live or to die.

Not that Simone Carrier or Steve Carson were in poor health. She was French and he was English. They were both fit and strong. On the other hand, she was suffering from a much more pitiable affliction than he, which became apparent in a matter of time, while he was suffering from an incurable disease – that of having fallen in love, and lost.

It had all become bitter and pointless. There was nothing more to do with his life – he would push himself to the limits on the icy tracks and granite peaks hanging over the Vale of Chamonix. Should it rattle his spirit – he would pay the price.

He knew nothing about women – nothing at all. They took advantage of him.

He managed to smile, swinging his climbing sack up onto his shoulders and setting off on the long trek up the Arve valley, the key to Chamonix. Having lost a woman, there was no going back. After three years' absence, he'd returned to restore his reputation. 'It's now or never,' on the icy pinnacles of Mont Blanc. If he had to serve sandwiches and drinks for a few hours each day to feed himself, then he would do it.

Simone Carrier threw open the curtains of her room in the Place Balmat at lunchtime. It was the centre of everything, and she was hours late. She'd seek out poor Marcel from the Bar Nash. That would be a sensible alternative. Then she thought about it a bit more – no, it wasn't – it would be more of the same – a pointless substitute.

Instead, she took the next available cable car to the top of the Aiguille du Midi – looked down on the whole town, strapped herself in, unfurled the paraglider at twelve thousand feet and ran as fast as she could over the edge of the precipice.

She didn't check to see if the cells of the canopy had filled with air. She knew it was the difference between life and death but the thrill of tempting fate and taking out her bad temper was too powerful to resist. She felt the sudden fall, followed by the huge uplift of air, as the soft, elliptical wing winched her back up from the depths and swung her out over the void.

It seemed that men had turned morality to their own behest. She pulled hard on the left-hand line, steering and veering off over the Bossons glacier, with its icy ridges. 'If it's right or wrong to take someone else's rights – I'll be judged on the same terms even if it kills me.'

She'd become known as the 'animal' by the men of the town. But she was more than that; she was as good or better than any man. She was wild and daring. Moreover, she was beautiful, on the outside at least, which drew men to her like bears around the honey pot.

'All or nothing,' she said. If it was to be nothing, then it would all be done in a grand way. She pulled erratically on the right-hand brake, felt the shudder from the wing, and the nylon guidelines soared effortlessly over the valley, seeking out a thermal which would lift her up to the heavens and far away from other people. You have to know exactly where to look, and she did. When she found one, she spiralled upwards in the warm air, alongside birds and insects, basking in the balmy uplift.

She could see Geneva on the north-western horizon. The Matterhorn stuck out like a horned snail to the east, and beyond the Valley Blanche and Mont Blanc itself, she could pick out the green meadowland of Courmayeur and the drift south into Italy.

Steve Carson was one of the best alpinists of his generation with a long list of difficult ascents to back up his claim; Simone Carrier was the best of her kind to fly and no one could disclaim her.

But what they couldn't see in that haze of sunlight, just over the frontier, was the adolescent figure of Sisto Carucci, prodding the dry earth with a short stick, frustrating – though not harming – the gallant efforts of myriad ants replenishing their supply lines. College had just broken up for the summer and Sisto was in love, for the first time in his life.

A feeling of such complete joy overwhelmed his young body and mind. Never had it been more important for him to construct the perfect sentence to explain what was going on inside him and never had he appeared more self-conscious in his actions or awkward in his speech.

Whenever the opportunity came to declare himself to the girl of his life, all he could do was to gulp down buckets of air, stammer out something unintelligible and stagger away into the recesses, completely drained. One day he would make it clear to his beloved how much she was a part of him.

Steve Carson did not know Sisto Carucci, as he plodded wearily up the Arve valley towards Chamonix. Neither did Simone Carrier, circling high up in the sky above, and they never really would – but in a strange way each of their lives would have a touching effect upon the other's.

But She's Beautiful

2

Steve Carson could hear the gentle patter of light rain when he pulled his head, snail-like, from the concrete pipe in which he'd spent the night. He settled down early and spent a long time mulling over the past and listening to the rumble of huge articulated lorries changing gear on the zig-zag slope up to Italy and then the Mont Blanc tunnel, lagging behind.

Then, before falling asleep, he'd heard the swish of something passing quite close overhead when he looked out of the end of the pipe, he was able to make out the winged shape of a paraglider circling above, before descending, smack dab, onto the roofs of the town. Only the mad or the suicidal would be foolish enough to attempt such a flight and landing after dark.

The fine rain had stopped falling. The sun was sweeping up over the Chamonix Needles. It tip-toed precariously onto the summit of the Midi, then launched itself into the valley. Condensation started to rise between the pines surrounding the town. Soon the ground was dry, and sunlight filled the whole crucible.

It was almost ten o'clock and lines of cars and coaches formed a long queue into the town. It was the same old Chamonix, perhaps even worse. Steve draped his sleeping bag over the concrete pipe to air, swallowed a chunk of stale bread and gulped down some tea, swimming with bits of grit from the stream.

'Here goes,' he thought, stuffing his sack and setting off into the town. It was a place he knew well and a valley he loved more than anywhere else in the world.

It was the end of June and though the height of the holiday season had yet to come, the streets were bright with the confetti of summer. The town had improved a lot since his last visit. So had the people, it appeared. There was a new wealth and a richer clientele. Bands of unwashed English climbers no longer wandered around in flip-flops with loaves of bread sticking out of the tops of their rucksacks.

He seemed out of place in this spruced-up town. So what? He hadn't come to mingle with anybody, least of all the tourists. His mind was fixed on the mountains. So were his eyes. He couldn't prevent himself from staring upwards to the line of jagged peaks stretching away to left and right on both sides of the valley.

At lunchtime, Steve Carson arrived at the Bar Nash, in the Place Balmat in the centre of the town. It had always been the gathering point for English-speaking climbers and for that reason he expected to hear a more familiar language. It was no longer the case.

Old Maurice was still there, sure enough, screwing up his burnt-out eyes behind the counter, but instead of stone floors and bare walls ringing to the sound of vulgar laughter, the whole establishment had been refurbished and a new breed of customer had moved in and replaced the dirty old crag rats.

Thinking better of it, Steve resisted the temptation to enter the bar. He dumped his sack at his feet, removed his boots and lowered himself onto a pink plastic chair at one of the outside tables. Someone from inside the bar came rushing up to him.

'We don't serve climbers with rucksacks anymore,' said a foppish little waiter.

'You'll serve me,' replied Steve Carson in impeccable French.

'Get rid of your bag!' said the waiter. 'Or move along yourself.'

'Go and seek Maurice!' said Steve.

'Monsieur Maurice, Monsieur Maurice,' gabbled the prissy waiter. 'We have a climber who refuses to leave the bar.'

'We are no longer a public bar, monsieur,' said Maurice, drawing up alongside Steve Carson. 'Now, we are a restaurant. As such, we reserve the right to… Steve, is it you?' continued Maurice, squinting hard. 'It is. You crazy Englishman! Marcel, *servez les autres*! Why didn't you say! We're all posh here now, but for you, I'll never get forget how you—'

'Maurice, I'm stuck,' said Steve. 'I need a pillow for the night.

'You're welcome, for as long as you like,' said the restaurateur splaying out his hands. 'Why didn't you tell me you were on your way? I could have prepared something.'

'Things have changed,' observed Steve, looking round the square.

'There are no more of your countrymen, if that's what you mean. It's no insult to you, my friend, but they were thieves and vagabonds – not true alpinists, like you. Do you remember the night they tried to steal all my roast chickens, outside, in the spit?'

'I remember,' smiled Steve.

'And they hated you because you were on my side. Are you surprised that we've cleared them all out?'

'They were just having fun. I need a few days' shelter.'

'Yes. Some fun! How about having your own room – for a few hours' work, each week? What do you say? I can make use of your shoulders. Yes?'

'You've got them.'

'Up there,' said Maurice, stabbing his finger towards the attic. 'My dear Steve,' he continued. 'My dear friend, you'll breathe some life back into the place. You've come to climb, non? Does Pascal know that you're back in town?'

Steve shook his head, picked up his sack and hauled it up to the top of the building. When he got there, he wasn't disappointed. The view from his attic window was magnificent. A panorama of rock faces and snowy peaks lay in front of him. The Chamonix Needles were still flooded with yellow light. A pink glow was about to be ignited halfway up the towering blocks of granite. This was where he lived – this was home!

He would be able to pick out unclimbed lines, trace them with his finger, execute them, unhindered by anyone else. That was Steve Carson's style. He nearly always climbed alone, as did Pascal, his long-time adversary. His mind was already floating in higher regions, when it was suddenly brought back down to earth and to the present.

'Don't you dare touch me!' resounded a woman's shrill voice from the window of the building on the opposing side of the alleyway, just three feet away.

'Mademoiselle!' cried a man in return. 'You give us no choice but—

'I give you no choice; you stand around all day waiting for a choice. That's what you mean, isn't it?' said a woman's irate voice.

When Steve Carson looked in the direction of the commotion, he saw two gendarmes trying to restrain a young woman, whose long black hair was blowing through the open window as violently as the head that was shaking it.

'Have you seen what they're doing?' she shouted, the moment she realised there was a witness to her predicament. 'Look they're pulling me.'

'Mademoiselle, it's not the first time we've had to arrest you,' continued the second gendarme. 'If you won't come voluntarily...'

'We have the right to question you,' said the first, a handsome man with a neat little moustache.

'You have no right to assault me, Brel… just because you can't get me to open my legs to you!' she yelled, at which point the two gendarmes glared across the open gap dividing them from Steve Carson and immediately loosened their grip on the young woman.

'Mademoiselle Carrier, be reasonable. We know it was you.'

'I'm not going to the gendarmerie. I detest you! You're all scum!'

'You're a danger to the whole town, as well as to yourself,' said one of the gendarmes.

'Leave me alone. Do something more productive. Go and seduce some young girls on the camp site. Collect the money from your women.'

'There's no point in insulting us, mademoiselle. We have our job to do,' said the gendarme with the tidy moustache. 'You were seen over the town last night. You landed on the flat roof again. People recognised your parachute.'

'Cons! Who recognised it? Which people?'

'The same ones. It was you. It's always you. You're reckless!'

'You're wrong. I wasn't even here last night. It's not true. I wasn't here – was I?' said Simone Carrier, staring across the alleyway, towards the Englishman. 'I was with him,' she continued, appealing to Steve through her big black eyes. 'Wasn't I.'

'Is that true, Monsieur!' said the other gendarme, suspiciously. 'Was she with you last night – at the very moment people allege that she was seen flying over the rooftops.'

Steve Carson hcsitatcd for a couple of seconds. 'If she was with me, she couldn't have been flying over the town,' he replied.

'You haven't answered my question, monsieur,' said the gendarme.

'I thought I had,' said Steve.

'Was she with you?'

'Of course – who else but me?'

'Where were you?'

'Not here,' said Steve.

'This is serious, monsieur. Don't play games with us. Where were you?'

'On the outskirts of town,' said Steve.

'Where?'

'In a pipe.'

'A pipe?' repeated the gendarme with a moustache.

'That's right.'

'What were you doing in this pipe?'

'What people normally do in a pipe.'

'Your French is very good, monsieur,' continued the gendarme. 'But don't trip yourself up. What are you? American?'

'If you must know, we were making love – I make love with everybody I like,' said Simone Carrier, coming to the rescue.

'You don't need to tell me,' said the gendarme. 'That's your game – did you even bother to find out his name before you got into this pipe with him?' smiled the gendarme. 'I would keep well away from Simone Carrier if I were you, monsieur,' he advised, leaning across the gap. 'She's well known in this town. One session with her and... well, I don't need to tell you.'

'*Salaud!*' spat Simone. 'You're no different from the rest.'

'And your vanity will put paid to you, Simone,' said the other gendarme who'd kept mainly quiet up until then.

'That's right,' said the moustachioed man. 'You, you too, monsieur. She could even be the death of you. What's your name? You have a look about you. Show me your passport, monsieur.' Steve held it out to him across the gap. 'Ah, *Anglais*,' said the gendarme, fixing his gaze upon the photograph. 'You look familiar to me. At least if I didn't know you before, I promise I'll remember you next time. Are you staying long in Chamonix?'

'Hard to say,' said Steve.

'Mmm. Well, you must understand that there's a price to pay for everything, especially for those who make the mistake of getting to know mademoiselle Simone Carrier.'

'That sounds threatening to me,' said Steve.

'Not from me,' replied the gendarme. 'She's the one who'll make you pay. You haven't heard the last of this, Simone,' he said, turning to follow his colleague from the room. 'We'll make further investigations. Keep yourself available, Mr Carson – if you please,' he added, in English. '*Bonsoir*, goodnight, ladies and gentlemen.'

As soon as she realised that the two gendarmes were no longer within earshot, Simone Carrier burst into laughter. 'Well,' she said, 'I suppose you expect me to thank you for your convincing performance!'

'They were right though, weren't they?'

'Yes, I admit it. Do you know how difficult it is to land a wing on a flat roof as small as this – at night? You've got to be good.'

'Or crazy.'

'What do I care? Me? You? Someone else? It's all the same to me.'

'You made me an accomplice in your deception. Doesn't that bother you?'

'You're wrong, mister Steve Carson. You let yourself become an accomplice. You didn't have to go along with my story. My name is Simone Carrier. I'm thirty-four years old and I'm no virgin. You can have no rights of passage over me – if that's what you think.'

'I'm not even hoping.'

'No,' she said, flashing her big black eyes. 'Besides, you English men are all homosexuals, aren't you?' she added. 'You were never a nation of lovers.'

'We're still around.'

'The great British Empire, I suppose.'

'We do just enough to keep the nation intact. The rest of

the time is spent bailing you lot out – once more if you count today.'

'Don't go,' said Simone, hearing a knock at the door. 'The pigs are back. Ah, cest toi Marcel,' she cooed, pulling a man towards the open window and embracing him in front of her new neighbour. It was the scrawny waiter from the Bar Nash. 'This is my lover Marcel,' she announced, presenting the bemused waiter while closing the windows, just a bit, behind her.

'We've already met,' said the waiter, recalling their brief encounter earlier that afternoon, 'Come on, Simone, you know I haven't much time. I have to be on again in an hour.'

Simone Carrier angled her head and smiled derisively across the gap that divided her from Steve Carson. Then she drew the curtains and closed the window, just enough for him to draw mental images of her when she was out of his sight.

But she carried the Englishman's rough and vital image to her bed, lay down with the useless waiter and cursed herself for being who she was. It was already too late for her, he imagined. 'She's a woman of the streets, but she's beautiful,' pulling the sheets over his head and trying to cut out the sound from the passageway. He'd escaped from one woman and run straight into another. Far from his thinking, perhaps, it was too late for both of them.

Someone Crying 3

For the next three days Simone Carrier opened her curtains, just a chink, and peered out to see if there was any sign of the Englishman who'd come, so conveniently, to her rescue. When it became obvious that his room was empty, she flipped her head, half-heartedly, and pretended to spit through the open window towards him.

Last night's storm had clattered all round the mountains; it had been volleyed from peak to peak, lighting up the buttresses like giant sets in an open-air theatre. Now that it had cleared, there was money to be made flying tandems down to the town with enterprising tourists.

The Vale of Chamonix was split into two distinct halves. The northern side rose to a height about eight thousand feet at the Brevent, with a line of jagged summits running eastwards.

Most of the death and drama took place on the southern side. It dwelt, quite naturally, in the spires of granite and the tongues of ice tippling down from Mont Blanc, at almost a couple thousand feet. This was Steve Carson's side of the valley.

Between the two halves lay the town itself, divided into small squares and linked by narrow streets. The buildings in the centre were made of stone and topped with an ornamental façade. The hotels and outlying chalets were built of wood in the traditional style and set off with window boxes, brimming with bright flowers. Through the centre of the town ran the Arve, a gushing river, fed by melting glacier water from the southern side of the valley.

Now that there was fine weather again, it was time for Simone to pack her paraglider and take the telecabine up to Planpraz, the launch pad for all beginners. When she got to the top, a female client was already waiting for her.

Simone strapped her passenger into the harness of the huge paraglider, gave careful instructions, then sprinted off the launchpad with her as fast as possible. She could feel the resistance of the wind as the multi-coloured canopy inflated above their heads and carried them both out into space.

Simone guided the great glider out over the valley, avoiding the black cables taking cabins up to the summit of the Brevent. She threaded the wing between other flyers, dotted about the sky, found a current of warm air, then spiralled upwards so that she could take a look at what was happening on the southern side.

Something dramatic was taking place on the Aiguille du Midi. The red rescue helicopter had been flitting about most of the morning.

At that same moment, Steve Carson was chopping his way up the Frendo Spur. Three days earlier, he'd got up at dawn and taken the rack railway up to Montenvers in an effort to forget the young woman who'd made such an impression upon him at their first meeting. It had been an impulsive decision. The mountains had turned nasty, and he found himself marooned in a crowded hut for two nights.

So he'd crammed his gear into his sack and moved lower down the mountain. Then he watched mighty thunderbolts chase each other along the crests of the needles and listened to the buzz of electricity zipping along the ridge. Her face had appeared in front of him again, in a shower of blue sparks and white light.

Simone Carrier frightened him. She was everything he was trying to forsake. But he couldn't forget her. She'd started to possess him from the moment he'd set eyes on her through the open window. Her black heart was already measuring up on him as it flew, from peak to peak, with the demons pitching in the storm.

Now he was halfway up the Frendo Spur. It was a classic mixed rock and ice climb – just what he needed to get himself back into condition. He'd regained his rhythm and concentration on the earlier slabs and chimneys, bulging with ice. He'd forgotten all about Simone Carrier and couldn't have guessed that her eyes were burning into him even then from the other side of the valley.

The sound of the rescue helicopter, swooping in on him, high up the ridge. Someone started to harangue him with a loudhailer. Did they think he was in trouble? He threw up his axe and waved it at them in defiance. Then he saw what all the fuss was about. At the foot of the final buttress of rock two climbers were trapped, after a night spent at the mercy of the storm. The helicopter could get no nearer and a rescue from above would take time.

When Steve Carson appeared, cramponning up the ridge, the two climbers could make only feeble attempts to wave to him. They were cold and hungry. He was warm and supple, after nearly three thousand feet of climbing. It was a nuisance, but he couldn't abandon them. They'd been right in the line of fire. He tied himself onto their rope.

The final wall was fierce. It had been blasted over with thin ice and was desperate, even for him. Two ropes' length later, he heard garbled voices and saw excited faces peering down from the belvedere above. Then a rope was dangled down to him and he tied into it, just as the difficulties eased.

'You old bastard!' shouted a voice from above, as Steve Carson's head appeared at the top of the climb, helmet removed. Steve raised an eyebrow and stared hard as the grizzly face with bear's whiskers poked out from the crowd of rescuers. 'Is this how you finish all your climbs?' asked the rough-looking man. 'Reeled in like a bloated whale?'

For a moment, Steve Carson found it difficult to respond. He despised rescuers even more than the people they rescued. But this man wasn't one of the team. 'What are you doing,' here he asked? 'This isn't your scene.'

'No more than yours,' replied the man. 'I was at hand.' Pascal Breton was a renegade – a brilliant alpinist who'd put up many of the new extreme climbs. He'd trained with the Compagnie des Guides, but they'd disowned him for putting the lives of his clients at risk. Now he was an independent guide.

Steve untied the rope and threw it onto the ground, while the rescuers continued to winch in the two climbers from below.

'Come on, *Anglais*, we'll cadge a lift down to the valley. Come to climb?'

'Maybe.'

'Come on, spill it, you aren't here for the weather – new routes?'

'Some.'

'With me?'

Steve shrugged his shoulders.

'Alone then. Okay,' grinned Pascal. 'It's been three years. We've been in hibernation for too long. Where are you staying – with Maurice?'

'Maybe.'

'That old bat! He's deserted us climbers. Chucked out the English – now he's after richer pickings.'

16

Steve could hear Pascal remonstrating with the pilot of the helicopter. 'Miserable bastard!' he moaned. 'Everything's money to these guys. Don't they know they're in the company of gods? Anyway, I've fixed it. He'll cram us in with those half-dead bastards you dragged up. Maybe you shouldn't have bothered. Come on, *Anglais* – relax. The brave look good when they smile. I'll meet you at the Alpenstock, any night this week,' shouted Pascal, making his getaway as soon as the helicopter had touched down.

A small group of police and ambulance people were waiting in the town. Steve looked sullen; he'd already forgotten Pascal's advice. Someone shoved a cassette recorder under his nose and asked him questions about the rescue.

'I don't speak French,' he lied, in the presence of the policeman whom he recognised as the one with the moustache from the encounter with Simone Carrier.

'So, you're the great hero?' said the gendarme, when the formalities had been gone through and he was walking beside him back into town. Steve Carson remained silent. 'Come, Mr Carson,' he added, 'you don't have to be modest with me. I know you speak French. Good publicity is hard to get. Why not make the most of it?'

'I climbed the ridge for myself,' he said. 'Not for anybody else's benefit.'

'It must be your mission in life?' said the policeman.

'What mission is that?' said Steve Carson.

'Coming to the rescue of other people. I've only met you twice and each time you played the part of the Good Samaritan.'

'I was in the right place at the right time.'

'Well – you won't have to worry about Mademoiselle Carrier again.'

'I'm not worried,' replied Steve, pricking up his ears.

'We've decided to let her go – as a special favour, you might say.'

'To whom?'

'Well, to me, to you,' replied the gendarme, smugly, 'to all those who shared – what shall we say – a pipe with her in the middle of the night.'

'It's nothing to me,' said Steve, disguising his interest.

'Well, she's a very charming girl, in many ways, don't you agree, Mr Carson? I seem to have upset you, by the look on your face. No, I mean there's no way we can make a case against her, now that you've provided her with an alibi. Besides, she's promised she won't do anything reckless again. I'll leave you here – buy a paper tomorrow,' he added, as he crossed the street. 'You'll like what you see. Yes, she's a charming little creature is Simone Carrier – for a while, that is. Well, au revoir, monsieur.'

Mr Maurice shouted a greeting as Steve Carson climbed past him and went up to his room at the top of the stairs. He should have been happy, but he wasn't. He felt unsettled and agitated.

He'd worn the same clothes for three days. He hadn't been able to wash, and a cold sweat had solidified on his bank. So, he stripped off, almost immediately, and sluiced away the grime. Then he shaved, put on a clean shirt and trousers, and combed back his over long hair.

Simone Carrier flicked back her long hair at about the same time, caught a glimpse of the Englishman in the mirror and span round involuntarily, with a gasp.

'You look just like an Englishman,' she said, gliding to the window and sticking out her chest.

'That's because I am one,' he replied.

'No imagination, no flair.'

'Uninspired,' he ranted.

'Dull,' said Simone.

'Predictable,' added Steve.

'Controlled, no sharp edges. In fact, boring.'

'*Je suis comme je suis*,' said Steve Carson, finally. 'Are we going to knock this thing backwards and forwards all evening?'

'Where have you been hiding for the past three days?' said Simone, angling her head.

'Here and there.'

'So don't tell me. I'm not all that interested in your social life anyway.'

'I've been on a trip.'

'That's what I thought,' said Simone, dismissively. 'You missed all the excitement up on the Midi.'

'Really – I always do.'

'Three climbers were stuck at the top of the Midi.'

'Only two, in fact,' said Steve Carson.

'Oh, you've heard? They only came down an hour ago. It's full of newcomers and gossipers.'

'Yes, you sound like a gossiper,' said Steve.

'I meant newcomer. I wasn't born here. I'm the type they gossip about. Perhaps you'll be one too.'

'I don't think they'd have much to say about me.'

'Don't be so smart, you know what I mean,' said Simone. 'I don't seem to get through to you, Mr Carson, do I? I'll try once more. What do you do? How long are you staying?'

'I ramble and scramble. I don't know how long I'll be here.'

'Have you a proper job?' she asked.

'Have you?'

'I fly people down from the mountains.'

'I take people up to the mountains.'

'Do you annoy people on purpose, Mr Carson?'

'It seems to come naturally when I speak to you. Do you fly?' he asked.

'I never have.'

'Then you can't be a climber, because those who climb also fly – or you don't keep up with the trend.'

'I'm English – remember? We're always a bit out of touch.'

'I'm getting bored with you, *Anglais*,' said Simone, half

turning. 'Besides I've got better things to do. Maybe we'll get through to each other, one of these days.'

'You never know.'

Steve Carson could observe everything from behind the counter at the Bar Nash. He could see Marcel's little bottom wriggling to and fro, as he served the customers in the restaurant. Steve wondered what Simone saw in him.

Marcel looked troubled and Steve Carson noticed that he was always peering towards the ground-floor entrance to Simone Carrier's apartment.

At about ten o'clock in the evening, someone appeared on the steps. He lingered a moment, squinted towards Simone Carrier's, then straightened his tunic and walked off across the square. A few seconds later, Marcel threw his napkin onto a table and disappeared out through the doorway of the Bar Nash.

'Marcel! Marcel!' cried Mr Maurice. 'Where the hell has, he gone? Steve, serve another bottle of red to number five, will you? This is the end. I've had enough of this pimp and his bloody prostitute!'

Steve Carson obeyed the instruction given to him by Maurice – then found himself bounding up the stairway to his room at the top of the building. He'd never been interested enough to listen in on anybody else's conversation in the past but this time he found it irresistible.

'You still haven't told me what Brel was doing here.'

'I didn't say he was here. You said it. You don't tell me what to do,' said Simone. 'I belong to myself. I always have and I always will.'

'You're shameless!' said Marcel. 'No wonder they call you the animal.'

'The women are jealous! The men can't tame me.'

'That's not the reason,' contradicted Marcel. 'It's because you're sick and depraved.'

'You know what to do, Marcel. After all, I'm not really your type, am I?'

'What do you mean? I thought you cared.'

'You called me your lover, the other day,' said Marcel.

'It suited my purpose. You've never been my lover, and you wouldn't have said so either if you didn't need to show you're still a man – even though you aren't!'

'What do you mean by that?'

'You know, the police, Pascal – everybody at the Alpenstock. Go home, Marcel – you're not like them – I've covered too long for you.'

'Go home you say. What about my parents. They know I'm a man. One day you'll die for your wickedness, Simone.'

'Oh, go on, Marcel – that's your problem. I've already told you – get out of here.'

Simone Carrier lay down on her bed and thought about the past. She was a relative newcomer to Chamonix, just as she'd told Steve Carson. Her real home was over the hills, in Provence.

As a girl, she'd always been mischievous. It was in her nature to giggle and to play silly pranks on people. She had a twinkle in her eye and an infectious love of life which affected everybody who knew her.

She'd been brought up on a farm. Her father had a vineyard. There were peach and olive trees all around the house. The sun shone down, all day, on the red earth, and as a child, she ran up and down the rows of vines, playing hide and seek with her best friend, Monique. She could hear her friend's voice still calling, so softly, to her from the past.

'Simone, where are you? Don't jump out on me again. What are you up to now?'

Simone smiled, then burst into tears. 'Oh, Monique,' she sobbed, tears flooding down her cheeks. 'I feel it now, just as much as I did then. It's so painful. Will I never forget? What can

I do to make up for that awful day? Forgive me,' she begged. 'Oh, Monique, please forgive my wickedness.'

Steve Carson stood by his open window, long after the argument between Simone and Marcel had ended. He thought he could hear someone crying across the alleyway. He tried to listen hard. No, it couldn't be. Perhaps it was only Maurice, down in the bar, telling Marcel that he no longer required his services.

Up in the Clouds

4

The weather was beautiful. Sunlight illuminated the wooded slopes of the valley. Steve Carson followed the ribbon of white water splashing down to the meadows with his binoculars. An unbroken thread led upwards to its source, in the shattered ribs of glaciers slithering down from the Chamonix Needles.

He trained his eyes on the whole range, scanning the peaks from left to right, wondering how such a site could ever have been unplanned in the whole of the universe. He traced the outline of the Frendo Spur, reclimbing it in his mind's eye, as he had in reality a few days earlier. What would be next, he wondered.

Then he heard Maurice calling to him from downstairs in the bar. Since the dismissal of Marcel, there was an even greater need of Steve Carson at the Bar Nash. Maurice knew that the Englishman was serious and dependable. It wasn't a perfect arrangement for the man who'd come to climb mountains, but with the proviso that he could take time off, when it was absolutely necessary to make an ascent, he agreed to do more.

There was no sign of Simone Carrier. In the morning, he could hear her moving around, preparing her equipment for flights down to the valley with her clients, but he could only guess which, of all the paragliders wheeling in the sky above, was hers. Besides, he didn't want to give her the impression that she was anything more than just an irritation.

In the evening, when she'd been grounded for the night, he was often working in the bar. She knew this but, despite walking past on one occasion, something he'd noticed but not acknowledged, he pretended he didn't exist.

On the third evening he was free for a couple of hours. He turned right from the Bar Nash and walked the few metres to the Place de Saussure, from which there was a good view of Mont Blanc. A statue of Dr Paccard and Jacques Balmat, the first ascensionists, had been mounted on a large block of granite surrounded by a splash of brilliant flowers. There was always a gang of people dashing around.

Steve liked to sit next to it at sunset and watch the shadow of the sun creeping up the Needles, until the last flames had flickered away and been extinguished on the snowy slopes beyond. A chill current of air rose from the Arve. It rushed past at an amazing speed, tempting the curious and the mad to jump in and follow it down to Geneva. Steve Carson got to his feet, crossed the bridge over the river and walked into the Alpenstock. It was time to fulfil an obligation.

'Ah, *Anglais*,' shouted Pascal Breton, as the quiet Englishman looked around him and picked out a group of independent guides, sitting in a cluster. 'Make space for a conquistador,' he continued, holding up a newspaper. 'Look, my friend – it's a picture of you.' Steve tried to appear modest, while Pascal waved the newspaper about in front of his face. In fact, it was the first thing that Maurice had thrown at him the morning after the rescue. 'Listen!' said Pascal, reading out the headlines and the best bits of the story for the benefit of his friends. 'Don't you love the adoration? Just a little bit, hey? Even you, *Anglais*?'

Pascal's ability to play to the crowd was one of the reasons Steve had put off their meeting at the Alpenstock for as long as he had. That and the new fascination he found for Simone Carrier. But nothing had developed so far as she was concerned. Now, it was time to find out from Pascal what had been happening in the valley during his three-year absence.

'*Cet homme*,' said Pascal, warming to his audience. 'This man is the coolest climber in the whole world. Not only that, he's also the most gifted and renowned alpinist of our time.' Steve Carson felt embarrassed. 'Except for one other!' cried Pascal, to the cheers of his countrymen.

'Who is this other man?' shouted a guide called Bruno.

'A humble man,' replied Pascal. 'A man whose exploits go unrewarded, because they remain unknown.'

'A fool – mmm. No, just a minute,' said Bruno. 'I've got it.'

'He's got it,' said Pascal, with bated breath. 'Tell us who it is.'

'It has to be you!'

'Ah! No! Whatever put that in your head?' exclaimed Pascal, while the rest pelted him with bits of bread and the rolled-up newspaper. 'Enough of this nonsense. Steve, mon ami, take no notice of us French. We're complete idiots. Let's get serious. Tell me. What is it to be? The Dru? The Grandes Jorasses? Not that pile of crap we found you on the other day.'

'I'm still working on it, Pascal.'

'I don't want to hear that from you, Steve. Is it the two of us together this time, side by side? What do you say?'

'Maybe. When I get fitter.'

'Listen, Steve,' whispered Pascal. 'Things have moved on quite a bit since we last saw you. Do you fly parapente? You call them paragliders, don't you?'

'No, but I've seen them flying about.'

'Then learn. That's where the future is. It's all speed now – as many major ascents as you can manage in a day. You climb to the top, fly down and move onto another. We've got something big going on the Dru. What do you say?'

'I don't know, it's not my style.'

'Come on, Steve. That's not the person I used to know. What about the challenge? You're like me – you won't be beaten, you've got to be the best. A climb together first, as friends. Then against each other – as combatants? Just as in the old days. Are you in?'

'Maybe.'

'When you say maybe, *Anglais*, I think you can only mean yes. Now, you must learn to fly.'

Steve began to realise just how much Alpine climbing had changed since his last visit. If you wanted to be right at the top, you had to keep up with new developments. Now he had a choice. He could carry on as a traditionalist, carving out harder routes on all the known faces, or he could join the band of climbers and flyers who made up the new generation.

Steve must have been thinking about it for a minute or two when, suddenly, he realised that everything had gone quiet. For a few seconds, an aura of complete silence descended on the room. Then, a crescendo of noise erupted all around him.

'The animal,' they shouted, in unison. 'It's the animal.' A great chorus of voices took up the chant. 'Animal! Animal! Animal!' they stormed, as Simone Carrier, not unused to the reception, entered the bar, nodding gracefully in acknowledgement and forcing her way through the crowd towards the group of French guides.

'Oh, this animal,' growled Pascal, standing and gyrating his hips on the spot. 'Simone, my little chou-chou,' he whimpered, taking the young woman's hand before kissing it and sweeping her up onto the table. 'A little kiss for the one who would throw himself from the top of the Dru if you would only grant him the smallest token of love.'

Simone appeared to be loving every moment of it. She looked more feminine than Steve Carson had ever seen her. She wore a lilac skirt, with tassels and a white common lace blouse, open at the front. Her skin was peach, her hair dark and lustrous. Her eyes were black and dazzling, and she displayed herself, tantalisingly, for all the stupefied men to crawl at her feet.

'Yet another kiss?' she replied. 'Is there no end to your grovelling, Pascal?'

'I'm dying, my little one. I won't last the night without the touch of your succulent lips against mine,' he said, placing his head between her feet and looking up into the recesses of her skirt.

'Once more then. After that, I'll take your money.'

'Mine as well?' said Pascal, climbing onto the table. 'But that's unjust, my sweet, don't we pay you enough already?' he continued, gathering her into his arms and smacking his lips against hers for what seemed an eternity to Steve Carson.

An enormous roar of approval went up around the room. Then, the rest of the guides jumped onto the table and tried to get their kisses – and a line of eager young men started to form around the room, ready to claim theirs.

'That's enough!' shouted Pascal when it seemed to be getting out of hand. 'Enough. The poor girl has hours of work ahead of her. We don't want to wear her out – do we?'

'We do! We do!' clamoured the mob.

'Okay. One more, by popular demand. But this time, it has to be something special, a kiss fit for a hero. Mademoiselle Simone? I present to you Monsieur Steve Carson, the intrepid angel of the Midi.'

Simone Carrier hadn't noticed the Englishman sitting in the midst of all the guides. When Pascal attempted to drag him up from his chair, her eyes met his for the first time. She looked startled and uncomfortable.

'No!' she gasped, as Pascal attempted to pull their two heads together to consummate the kiss. 'Not him. Not him!'

'Not him! Why? He's not so bad, for an Englishman. Come on, Simone, you're embarrassing him.'

'No! I won't do it,' she screamed. 'Leave me alone! Let me go!'

'Do you know who this is?' shouted Pascal. 'You insult our guest. This man saved the lives of two wretched climbers on the Midi, singlehandedly – and you refuse him a kiss, Simone. Where's your generosity? You've given much more for less.'

Then someone shoved the crumpled newspaper with a picture of Steve Carson right in front of her eyes.

'It is you!' she gasped.

They both stared deeply into each other's eyes and in that single moment, they knew. Simone broke free from the hands that constrained her without another word. In an instant, she'd leapt from the table and raced out into the street before anyone could think about stopping her.

'Your ugly face doesn't seem to fit,' said Pascal. 'I've never seen her react in such a way. Do you know her? She lives across from you.' Steve Carson shook his head. 'What is it then? A mismatch? Bad vibes?'

'Bad breath,' said Steve.

'Bad something,' grumbled Pascal. 'Don't worry, she'll come round. She goes like a rabbit – for me. I'll give her a piece of what she wants tonight. Come back tomorrow. I'll make you a present of her. When you've had enough of it, we'll go up a real present,' he said, pointing towards the Dru.'

Shortly afterwards, Steve Carson walked out of the Alpenstock. It was dark and the streets were full of late-night smells. The restaurant and forecourts were thick with people and a three-piece band was playing folk music to a crowd of onlookers. Steve bought a pancake and joined them. But his mind was fixed firmly on the beautiful young woman who was regarded as common property by all the men of the town. When he arrived at the bar Nash, Monsieur Maurice was pleased to see him.

'Steve,' he smiled, with relief. 'I'm all in – exhausted. Will you stay and look after the bar?'

'Has anyone entered the doorway over there?' he asked in reply.

'A thousand people, day and night,' said Maurice.

'What about in the last few minutes? Any men? A guide?'

"Do you think I sit here with a note book and say: *Yes; now it's your turn, Marcel and then it's Brel's and then Pascal's and – just wait- Steve wants to go in next!*"

'You said it right,' Maurice said. 'Spot on!'

'Yes, I have an answer, Steve. Don't get involved with loose women. Do you think I haven't got things to watch out for, with my poor eyes?'

'Are you going to tell me or not?'

'Tonight, there's been no one,' replied Maurice. 'Tomorrow, who knows – maybe the whole world. Or perhaps it's just too early for trade to begin.'

Steve hung about in the unlit bar, long after the last customers had left, his gaze fixed rigidly on the downstairs entrance to Simone Carrier's apartment block. At three o'clock in the morning, he crept upstairs to his room and stood next to the shadowy window for a long time, unable to go to bed.

It took a lot to unnerve Simone Carrier. She'd run the gauntlet, frequently, in the Alpenstock, playing the part that was expected of her, with conviction. She enjoyed teasing and tormenting the men. How stupid they were. If they thought that putting her on a pedestal would give them a better chance of breaking through the barrier, they were wrong. To Simone, it was all so much froth.

For some reason, the Englishman was different. His thoughts and feelings appeared unreadable to her. He'd helped her get out of a difficult situation, but he hadn't thrown himself at her and he hadn't expected any reward. Maybe that was why he lingered in her mind when he was absent, and why she resented him more and why she had the potential to feel something much deeper for him. Perhaps that was also why she'd gone to pieces when Pascal had suddenly dragged him unexpectedly in front of her.

It wasn't like her to go to bed early, but she had that night, anxious to forget her humiliation. The day after, she'd get back onto the wire and do something daring, before she lost her nerve altogether. She'd dress up as she never had before, show more of herself and stun them all into submission.

Her head looked so peaceful and childlike on her pillow. Her black hair fell in locks around her shoulders and a few strands covered her face. When she stared, momentarily, to sweep the strands out of her eyes, there he was, looking down at her.

'You,' she whispered, as if she'd been expecting him all along. 'What do you want? It's the middle of the night. Haven't you embarrassed me enough already?'

'I'd never do that,' he said.

'It isn't done, breaking into people's homes. I could call the police and have you arrested.'

'You'd be in more danger from them than from me.'

Simone suppressed a smile. 'How did you get in here?'

'I climbed in from the alleyway.'

'Oh, yes, the angel of the Midi. It's a long way down. You could have been killed.'

'Would it have been much of a loss?'

'Okay, you've had your fun. Why are you here?' she asked. 'Still hoping to collect on your winnings?'

'That was misjudged!' he remarked.

'So? Are you about to give me a lecture on how to take care of myself? No, thank you!'

Steve was going to say something else altogether, but the sharpness of her rebuke prevented him from saying it.

'Well, actually, I need someone…'

'Well?'

'I wondered if you'd teach me how to fly,' he stammered.

'Wow! What?' she exploded. 'You wake me up, in the middle of the night, to ask me that? Who do you think you are? I might have had someone staying.'

Carson was afraid of his real sentiments. They were lost in his mind. It was too late to say them now. All he could say was, 'I just thought that…'

'I bet you just thought – yes, I would do what you wanted – and that came down to flying. Men have wanted me for much more and if you want to talk to me about a business arrangement, do you mind waiting until morning? Look – get back on your own side,' she said, jumping out of bed and pushing him towards the window. 'Tough luck if you don't make it this time – it's a long way to fall!'

'Wait,' he implored her, when he already had one leg dangling over the void. 'That's not why I came at all.' The possibility of a free fall made him speak with more urgency.

'Then why?' she demanded.

'Because of you, I couldn't stop myself.'

'Go on.'

'I think we could get on a lot better. I'm sure of it – tonight, I saw something in you I'd never seen before.'

'Are you sure you aren't making it all up?'

'Yes, I am sure. You know too,' Steve was pushing it hard, for him.

'You know what they say about me,' she said. 'You know what they call me.'

'I don't care. I've seen something else in you.'

'You should care. What they say is true. I could land you in a lot of trouble.'

'I'm a big boy now,' he replied, enjoying the joke. 'I've seen trouble before. I know how to handle myself.'

'You don't know what you're saying,' she said, taking hold of his left arm in both hands and leading him back towards her bed. 'Okay, you can stay a bit, if you want to,' unsure of his promise. 'You can hold me – just hold me. Nothing else. If you can manage that, who knows? I might just teach you how to fly, after all.'

'I'm up in the clouds already,' said the astonished rock climber.

You'll Have to Find Out

5

Monsieur Maurice repositioned the tables and parasols in front of the Bar Nash. Then he walked across the Place Balmat to treat himself to an ice cream. Sunlight was glinting on the windows of the confectioner's opposite and a procession of tourists kept obscuring his view of the couple walking up the hill to the telecars. He screwed up his eyes even more tightly to see if he could confirm the suspicions he'd held for the past few days.

A moment or two later, Raymond Brel, the gendarme with the neat moustache, descended the steps of the gendarmerie. He too was distracted by the sight of the two individuals passing in front of him. He tried to smile to himself, but he had to confess that something inside was affecting his composure. He'd never really understood why he wanted to destroy the happiness of other people. He just did. It can wait.

'You're more frank than I am,' she admitted. 'I wouldn't dare tell you everything I've done in my life.'

'I'm not normally so open,' said Steve Carson. 'For some reason, I'm shy, especially with women, but it's easier with you because you're so open. We've lived in a world of our own these last few days – at least I have. I don't get it,' he added, brushing his fingers through his thick hair. 'I can say anything to you.'

'That's one of the reasons married men give for visiting other women. The wife doesn't understand them.'

'I tell you what I'm thinking because you understand me.'

'That's something else they're supposed to say.'

'You try hard to put me off you at times, Simone,' he said. 'Here, give me the sack.'

'I'll carry it myself, thank you. I just want you to realise what you're getting into with me.'

'How can I forget? You tell me every day,' said Steve.

'You couldn't really have believed in love every day, could you, or you would never have walked out on her.'

'I never walked out on her – in the end I was shoved out,' he admitted. 'She had other things on her mind.'

'How did I not have other things on my mind?' asked Simone.

'I don't. I just feel. I just feel you're looking for something different – like me.'

'It might be just a cover. Most women still want to get married and have babies.'

'You don't,' he told her.

'No, I'm just the animal, I suppose.'

'I didn't mean that, Simone,' he said, apologetically.

'Maybe I do want babies,' she said. 'Maybe I want a husband and lots of kids, just like all the others.'

'If you do you go about it in a very odd way.'

'I didn't say I did want that,' she snapped. 'I said, maybe I did.'

'I don't think so,' he persisted. 'You could have had it if you'd wanted it. You've had enough men.'

'How dare you say that?' said Simone aggressively. 'I haven't told you that – besides—'

'You're beautiful, they all worship you – you know it.'

'They all desire me – it's not the same!'

'It's more than that. You've got real power. If you'd really wanted something permanent, you'd have got it by now. Most women have a mission in life. That's why I lost my first one. They have to fulfil. You don't. You don't look to your belly; you aim for the sky just as I do.'

'Well, alright, let's aim for the sky, Steve Carson,' said Simone, as they arrived at the ticket office. 'Come on. We don't pay; I have a contract for the summer.'

She dumped the huge bag containing the parapente into the next cabin, jumped in herself, then pulled Steve in after her.

'I hate this bit,' he told her, holding on to his stomach, as the small cabin lurched between the support columns.

'What? You afraid of the drop?'

'Absolutely! I'm even more nervous about strapping myself into this thing,' he said, giving the glider a kick with his boot.

'Don't you trust me?'

'I don't trust anyone. I like to be in control, like my old girlfriend. It's good to be in control of your own destiny. But this is something I have to do apparently, to keep up with Pascal and the others. How long have you known him?'

'A couple of years. Besides, how old are you?' Simone said.

'I'm thirty-six, two years older than you. They say you get to halfway when you reach thirty-five.'

'Then I'll never get there – I'm too young. Anyway, talking of Pascal, I taught him everything he knows.'

'That could mean a lot of things,' he smiled.

'I meant paragliding; you couldn't teach him anything else. Why don't we forget him. He's in the past now.'

'You know what he's like. He's ego-centric, like most of us are. He thinks he knows it all,' admitted Steve. 'He's popular enough

– even with you. From what they say, everybody assumes you belong to him.'

'Don't, Steve,' she begged, buttoning his lips with the tip of a finger. 'I belong to nobody. Don't keep fishing around. We are only at the beginning. Don't spoil it before we get off the ground.'

The cabins arrived, one after the other, at Planpraz, the highest point of the circuit. On the other side of the valley, the red clockwork train was busy ferrying tourists back and forth through the pine forest to Montenvers and the Mer de Glace.

The view of the Mont Blanc massif was stunning. A line of granite pillars chewed up the skyline. Vast snowfields slipped silently into the glaciers. It was love and destruction rolled into one, heaven and hell at peace with the sun.

'We'd better get going,' said Simone, 'before we decide to spend the day lying on our backs.'

'That would be even more dangerous,' muttered Steve.

They walked up the stony track to the launch site, where a group of tourists had gathered around the flyers, preparing their canopies for take-off.

'Hell fire!' cried Steve. 'Do I have to take my maiden flight in front of this lot?'

'We won't get airborne if you don't.'

'I can't perform in public, I'm a very private guy. Can't we go somewhere a bit quieter? Preferably closer to the ground.'

'Listen, softie, nobody's interested in you. All you have to do is run – I'm the one who'll get us off the ground.'

'And if you don't?'

'If I don't you won't have to worry about tomorrow. But I will! Don't you remember how we first met – with the police?'

'Oh yeah. If I'd listened to those guys I'd have been out of this by now. I've got a feeling this isn't my kind of thing at all,' said Steve. 'How did the other chap do.'

'Don't ask – he's good at everything.'

'I guess he is.'

'Besides,' said Simone, 'you aren't flying solo. This is just a test flight to give you an idea of what it's all about.'

They rolled the paraglider out on the ground behind them. Then she started to examine it for damage to the lines and fabric. It was much bigger than Steve had imagined. From below, paragliders appeared as mere dots circling high over the town but, close up, this one was nearly forty feet wide and ten feet deep.

'Here, put this on,' said Simone, passing Steve a helmet.

'Do I have to?'

'This is serious. I'm wearing my instructor's cap now, and you'll do exactly as I tell you.' Then she strapped him into the dual harness and gave him his instructions.

'Right, keep your hands clear of the lines. Take hold of the harness and don't let go till I tell you. We take off into the wind, you've got to run like mad and don't stop, even when I've left the ground after you. Understood?'

'Yes, captain. Am I allowed a final word?'

'Go on.'

'Maybe I fall in love with you, and then I get killed,' he murmured.

'That could be true – they call it love on the rebound,' she replied, making the final checks. Simone felt a warm glow in her heart as the breeze blew gently up the slope towards the ramp. 'This is it,' she said, sweeping up the canopy behind them, steadying it above their heads and beginning the run down the launch pad. 'Come on! Go for it!'

As they sprinted towards the abyss, Steve Carson could feel the adrenalin racing through his body. He took a long, deep breath, grasped a tight hold of the harness and waited to meet his fate.

'Well, what do you think?' she said, as they drifted out, high above the valley.

'I'm delirious,' he said. 'This is a real high.'

'No more worries – you haven't seen anything yet!'

'I'm in the palm of your hand. Make sure you keep me there!'

'I'm going to break off and soar along the ridge,' she said, pulling on the right-hand steering line and turning towards Geneva. 'Can you see those birds overhead? They've hooked a thermal; so can we.'

Soon, they were rising above the summit of the mountains on the north side of the valley. Then they were looking down on the Aiguille du Midi, with its great snowy buttresses, shining in the midday sun. 'Remember that – you climbed it not long ago and saved those unfortunates.'

'I know it – well, well, we're looking at it from a different angle – it's out of this world,' he marvelled. 'If Pascal can do it, so can I.'

'It's not this one,' she said, soaring even higher. 'It would put Pascal in his place.'

'No, I know, it's way over on the Dru – I'd have to get pretty good at it.'

'With several test runs from me, what else do you want?'

'Let's take a look at it now.' Simone kept circling and making figures-of-eight movements within the thermal. Then she levelled off.

'I didn't realise how little effort you had to make to get so high up in the world. We're higher than the summit of Mont Blanc. It's incredible!'

'One day soon, we'll fulfil a vision of mine,' she said.

'What's that?'

'To spend a night on top, all alone – just the two of us.'

'It's freezing cold at night,' he told her.

'We'll build an igloo, right on the very summit, and keep each other warm.'

Simone brought the glider out of the thermal at about sixteen thousand feet. They started to sink almost immediately.

'I'm getting drunk,' he said. 'My head's reeling already.'

'It's lack of oxygen – or maybe you're just a bit soft in the head. We'll fly downward and lose a bit of height.'

They picked up speed and glided quickly over the town, following the Arve to the east. Then Simone pulled on the right-hand steering line and the canopy turned gracefully over the Mer de Glace glass in the direction of the Dru.

'Oh, Lord!' he cried, recovering his inspiration for climbing. 'Have you ever seen anything as imposing as that? Let's have a real look – bring us closer.'

Simone found lift again, almost immediately, in the mass of warm air rising from the sweltering granite and the canopy drifted slowly across the west face of the Dru.

'Look,' shouted Steve. 'There are climbers all over the Bonatti Pillar. Can't you get closer?'

'The wind does funny things close to a mountain. It could blast us into the rock or shoot us over the top and dump us.'

'It's amazing!' continued Steve. 'Bonatti must have been one hell of an alpinist to climb it solo. Hold on a minute. They aren't on the Bonatti – it's a new line going up the smooth face to the left. I could almost reach out and...'

Then they saw a hand waving and a voice calling to them three-quarters of the way up. 'Ooo-eee! Ooo-eee! C'mon! Simone! Simone! *C'est toi.*'

'He's calling your name,' said Steve.

'It's Pascal. He's putting up a new route on the Dru. Everybody knows.'

'Everybody who's in the know,' said Steve.

'Simone! Salut! Make room for me tonight. I'm coming home,' roared Pascal. 'We're gonna find that little creature again.'

'How does he know it's you? He can't make you out from here.'

'He recognises my glider.' She spoke. 'Besides, I told him I'd be teaching you to fly.'

'When did you tell him? You've been with me for days.'

'I often bump into him on the hill. I said we might fly past if conditions were right.'

'So, he knows it's me, tied up in this nappy.'

'I suppose so,' replied Simone.

'And he can still say the things he's just said to you?'

'Oh, Steve,' said Simone. 'Pascal's a one-off. He always says things like that to me. It's meaningless.'

'Why didn't you tell him about us when you bumped into him?'

'I don't know, maybe I did. It may not last – you might have objected.'

'Or maybe you wanted to carry on playing the field?'

'I haven't thought about it,' replied Simone, coldly.

Simone took the giant canopy upwards over the summit of the Dru. 'I always like to look south from the top of the peaks,' she said, in an attempt to start up conversation again. 'I imagine if I get high enough, I'll be able to see the farm, in Provence where I was brought up. I'd like to take you there one day. That makes two things we still have to do.'

'Just get me down from here,' said Steve.

Simone swept in an arc over the Mer de Glace. Then, she flew in ever-decreasing circles until she was able to bring the glider down in a field just outside the town. Any worries Steve might have had about the landing were soon forgotten.

'Steve,' she said, taking hold of his hand. 'You don't have the right to treat me like this. Pascal means nothing to me. Neither does anyone else. It's all you now.'

'How many times have you given that little speech, I wonder?'

'I've told you it's all in the past,' she promised.

'The past can't be wiped out as easily as I thought; I found that myself. It's all around us. Who know if it's even in the present?'

'You knew it wouldn't be easy,' she said.

'I can't go on watching them pawing you about and chanting

that other thing, night after night, not knowing what kind of pictures are going through their heads, or yours, every time they see you. I thought I could live with it, but I was wrong; I made a mistake.'

'You've certainly sobered up since we flew over Mont Blanc,' she remarked. 'We've gone from the bottom to the top and right back down to the bottom again in just about an hour. What about the flying? You need to learn if you are going to compete with Pascal.'

'I'm already competing with Pascal. What do I owe you?'

'Steve, you know better than that.'

'Tell me,' he said, 'what is it about this let's just hold each other thing with you? Is that the starting point for everybody – or do some people get there quicker than others?'

'You'll just have to find out,' she said while packing up the equipment and making for the town.

You're Still Interested

6

Anybody who has made the kind of statements uttered by Steve Carson to Simone Carrier will realise just how difficult it is to go back on them a day later, when the feelings which inspired them have melted away.

The morning after, he felt completely drained. The trouble was, he'd had very little experience of women. At thirty-six years of age fate had marked him out for bitter involvement with a femme fatale and now he was feeling the pain.

Simone Carrier was no happier. She'd created a certain image of herself in settlement for a greater sin. At the time when love had broken through her defence, she was obliged to go on paying the price. Now, she had to harden herself once more and return to being the 'animal' everyone referred to her as. It was a heavy blow to take.

'Raymond Brel tweaked his moustache at the ground-floor entrance to Simone Carrier's apartment, until he was sure that his presence had been noted by everyone watching from the Bar Nash opposite. Then he straightened his uniform as usual and disappeared out into the street.

Monsieur Maurice rubbed his eyes and looked straight at Steve Carson before saying, 'Well, don't say I didn't warn you, my friend. At least she's more honest than most.'

'What do you mean?' said Steve, stabbing the counter with a bread knife.

'They all have the makings of it, but that one – she's bold. Everything's out in the open with her. Stick to your mountains. There's a danger up there too, but not half as much as down here.'

'I'll get on back on track.'

'Take a couple of days off. Go up to the tops and find yourself again. There are more mysteries waiting to be solved up there than anywhere in the universe. Go away a child and come back a man. Forget this woman.'

'I will, Maurice. I will,' he said, responding to his host's eloquence.

'In the meantime, bring up some red from the cellar.'

Steve Carson gave Maurice a weak smile and opened up the wooden trap, built into the floorboards of the bar.

Just before dark, he took a deep sigh, resisted the temptation to peer across the alleyway into Simone's flat and descended the stairs to the street. He must have done it completely in time with Simone because, just as he was about to come under the glare of the spotlights hanging over the entrance to the Bar Nash, the glass door to Simone's apartment block started to open and she emerged into the square.

She was dressed more demurely than usual and moved with rather less elegance. But she was still seductively dark and stunningly beautiful.

His original intention had been to meet up with Pascal and his rowdy friends at the Alpenstock. But the appearance of

Simone forced him to change his plans and he set off, meekly, in pursuit of her.

She left the Place Balmat by the Rue Joseph Vallot. All the souvenir shops were still open, and the street was teeming with tourists, choosing postcards and licking ice-creams. The chairs and tables of the roadside restaurants were all occupied and a band of copper-skinned flautists from Peru was serenading the crowd. For a few moments Simone stopped, closed her eyes and listened to the sounds.

Then she continued along the Rue des Moulins, until she came to the bridge spanning the Arve. She peered into the fast-running river, crossed the bridge and continued to the Place du Mont Blanc. It was wide and almost empty. By the time Stephen Carson had managed to cross the square without being spotted, she'd completely disappeared down one of the narrow alleyways, leading to several private chalets hidden away in the trees.

'Another client?' he wondered.

It was soon pitch dark. The beacon on top of the Aiguille du Midi was shining down to the valley. It was the only light he could see. He walked back, disconsolately, to the Bar Nash.

'How are you feeling?' said Maurice. 'Better?'

Steve nodded. He felt awful. He knew what it was like to go from near-indifference to profound suffering in rapid succession. His mind was bombarded by the most perverse images of Simone, and the more he tried to rationalise it, the more it tormented him.

Somehow, he managed to get through the night and the whole of the next day. Monsieur Maurice kept inviting him to take time off. He would, when it was worth it, but what was the point, just then? He was marginally better off working and trying to cope with the world.

In the evening, he resolved to go to the Alpenstock, no matter what happened. But he hung about in a corner of the bar, telling himself he'd do one thing but knowing he'd do another.

When the door handle eventually turned and she emerged, his heart beat even faster and he had to struggle hard to catch his breath. This time he wouldn't lose her trail, wherever she went. She took the same path as the night before and he followed, stealthily, not far behind.

A few metres beyond the Place du Mont Blanc, a driveway turned up to the right. Simone glanced behind her, stepped into the shadows and disappeared. Then she noted the door and for an instant her face was bathed in yellow light, as the door was opened, then closed, returning the porchway to darkness.

A minute later, Steve Carson was crouching beneath the open window of the chalet, trying to listen to the low sound of the conversation coming from inside.

'You look charming tonight, Simone,' said an older man's voice. 'Have you had a busy day?'

'There's plenty of work if you want it,' she replied.

'And you do, of course, if you want it.'

'When I feel up to it, I need the money.'

'Don't worry, there are ways and means.'

'You do more than enough for me already,' said Simone. 'You're my anchor in the world when things get tough.'

'Thank god someone as lovely as you can still turn to an old man for comfort,' said the voice.

'You aren't an old man to me,' said Simone. 'Far from it; you're crammed with youth and vitality.'

'Oh! My god, you'll make all the young men jealous if you say things like that.'

'It's true, if only other men were as good as you. This time I thought that—

'Yes, I know,' said the man. 'Sit yourself down, before you get upset again. I'd better close the shutters or we'll both be waking up in the night covered in mosquito bites.'

The man walked towards the window, unhooked the catch on the shutters and closed them from within. There was complete silence immediately and the only noise Steve Carson could hear was that of a distant stream tumbling down from above.

Steve felt confused; he didn't know what to make of the conversation. Who was the man? What part did he play in Simone's life? How intimate were they? Was she going to spend the whole night with him? It sounded like it. The more he thought about it the more he came up with tortured solutions to the questions. What was worse, he couldn't solve any of it by banging on the door and demanding answers to his questions or even hanging about outside the window to see what would happen. The mental imagery only increased his suffering.

Ten minutes later, Steve Carson feigned light-heartedness and walked into the Alpenstock, as if his anguish were at an end.

'Ah, *Anglais!*' shouted Pascal. 'You're lucky, we've just got back from the Dru.'

'Success?' said Steve, slapping him on the shoulder.

'Defeat! The rock was as smooth as glass – no placement for pitons and not enough time for bolts. Nobody could have done it! Not even you!'

'I agree, it looked hard,' said Steve.

'How would you know, my friend?' said Pascal. 'It's not the old Bonatti route. That fell down a long time ago. This line's further left and completely untouched. Does it appeal to you?'

'Maybe, it's my kind of thing.'

Pascal looked at Steve oddly and said, 'Next time then – but you don't fly. A pity. When we realised it was impossible to go on, do you know how long it took us to get down back to the town?'

'Tell me.'

'Seven minutes! Seven minutes from being a rope's length from the top of the Dru, to landing back in the town. If you'd been with us, we'd have had to abandon you. When are you going to get started?'

Obviously, Pascal hadn't noticed Steve in the paraglider –

and Simone hadn't told him. That put a different slant on the argument altogether. 'I'll be up shortly,' said Steve.

'Who are you with?'

'You know,' he said, but without giving it away at that moment.

'Is it Simone?' said Pascal knowingly.

'...Yes, of course,' he had to tell him, knowing Simone's openness.

'Wow! She doesn't waste much time – the animal! Hey, she's mine! She didn't tell me about you. I should have guessed. She's superb!' he continued. 'Good value for money – not a bad teacher either,' he guffawed. 'Have you had anything else out of it?'

'No, oh, come on, Pascal, don't go on about it.'

'Don't go on about it! Are you kidding me! Some pay, others get it for nothing. You can't help being English – you lack being a bourgeois! Don't worry. I always say a good shit is better than a poor shag. I'd give her one now if I weren't so knackered. Listen, when you're ready for the Dru give me a shout.'

He was more confused than ever. If Pascal had been telling him the truth, it appeared he knew nothing of Steve's flying lessons with Simone. What was she up to? Was she telling Pascal one thing and him another? Was she playing games with them? Was she endeavouring to make one or both of them jealous? The more he tried to sort it out, the more tangled up it all became.

At midnight, there was a light in Simone's bedroom. He hadn't looked across the alleyway for two days, so he couldn't know whether it was a light she'd left on intentionally, even though she was still out, or whether, in fact, she was back. He didn't have the courage to find out.

The next night, he waited for Simone to resume her evening ritual, with the intention of following her to the remote chalet once again. But she didn't come out at the usual time. He ran upstairs and noticed that her bedroom light was still on. Perhaps she was still at home, or maybe she'd gone out earlier. It was possible she hadn't even come back from the night before.

Not long afterwards, Steve found himself crossing the Place du Mont Blanc. A few seconds later, he was standing in the porchway of the mountain chalet, trying to make up his mind whether to knock or not, and the door suddenly opened. Standing before him was a tallish, lean man with silvery hair.

'Ah, monsieur! You made me jump. I was expecting someone else. What can I do for you?'

'I'm a friend of Simone Carrier, I thought she might be here,' Steve replied. 'I thought she might…?'

'Here?' said the man, completing the sentence for him.

'Yes, well, I…'

'I thought that might be her now,' said the elderly gentleman. 'Come in, we can wait for her together.' Steve entered the comfortable chalet, with its natural, stained wood and rustic furnishings. There were several woollen rugs covering the floorboards and the walls were lined with bookshelves and tastefully chosen ornaments and pictures. 'I was just about to pour myself a glass of something,' the man said. 'Would you care to join me? Wine, pastis, fruit juice?'

'Wine, please,' said Steve.

'Ah, an Englishman who appreciates wine – you are an *Anglais*, aren't you?' said the man.

'Is it so obvious?' said Steve.

'I wasn't being distasteful,' said the man. 'Just making it enough to be attractive. I suppose you must also be curious about me. Why not sit down?' Steve chose an armchair in a corner of the room. 'Does Simone know that you've come here tonight?'

'Not exactly.'

'Do I take it that means no?' asked the man.

'Yes – in a way.'

'Then might I ask you how you found out about this place – how she visits me here?'

'I followed her.'

'Not tonight, evidently, because she hasn't arrived.'

'Last night and the night before,' replied Steve, quite happy to be able to tell the truth.

'Then it must be very important to you to know why she comes here,' said the old man, passing him a glass of red wine.

'Yes, it is.'

'Because she hasn't told you about me – has she?'

'No.'

'And you must be wondering who I am?'

'I am wondering – I'm lost in this world of make believe.'

'Because Simone has a certain reputation in this town.'

'Yes,' said Steve. 'Very good. You understand much better than I.'

The elderly gentleman smiled, as if the suspicions held by his visitor might, in other circumstances, have been regarded as a compliment. 'You'll forgive me if I say that you look suspicious. I have the impression that you regard me as a threat.' Steve made no reply. 'Take a long look at me,' he continued. 'You flatter me if you believe that someone as young and beautiful as Simone would show any interest in an old goat like me.'

'Why not?' said Steve. 'I've seen young women with older men. It's a pretty good deal all round – a bit of a meal for you and a whole lot of money for her.'

'Oh, Steve,' groaned the old man. 'You dishonour not only Simone and me but you, too, by even suggesting such a thing.'

'How do you know my name?' asked Steve.

'How do I know your name?' repeated the old man. 'I've heard it a thousand times over these past few days. I've heard the story of how she met this wonderful Englishman, by chance, and how he changed her whole life in a matter of days. I'm disappointed in you, Steve,' he continued. 'You must not know Simone as well as she thought she knew you, though I must say, I think her faith in you appears to have been misplaced.'

'What part do you play in it?' enquired Steve.

'My part? Why, I'm a friend, of course – an old friend, though, like you – and one, it seems, who has much more clarity of vision.'

'I can see clearly enough as it is,' replied Steve Carson. 'I see people leaving her apartment. I see them again, in the street and in the bars. There's nothing wrong with my eyesight, it's my brain that needs examining.'

'You're right, Steve. No, I'm not being insulting. You're different, I can see that. You're sincere. You wouldn't be here if you weren't. But you've got it all wrong. Let me tell you something, my young friend. You came here to confirm a painful suspicion. In fact, I suspect you've rather enjoyed the pain. You see me as insane or something – it's you who need to look in the mirror, my friend.'

'Really? You know that much. It happened to me once before. The pain is unbearable.'

'Well, maybe insane is a bit strong, but you certainly indulged it, and I did detect a sense of disappointment on your part in realising that you were wrong. You thought you knew the truth about Simone? But you were mistaken, certainly in relation to me. I may equally be mistaken about her, but I doubt it. In fact, it's possible the only guilt attached to Simone is in the image which surrounds her.'

'Which she is responsible for,' said Steve.

'Agreed! But there may be reasons for that.'

'What reasons?'

'I can't tell you,' replied the old man. 'I don't know – things from the past, maybe. Try a bit harder.'

'I can't,' said Steve. 'It's too painful. I've suffered enough already.'

'But you came back. You're still interested. Besides, you aren't the only one who's suffered. So has she. I've seen it for myself. You're the best chance she has in the whole world,' he continued. 'You too, perhaps – don't waste it!'

She Held Him Close

7

Simone Carrier adjusted her bulky climbing sack, looked back along the track and waited for her companion to catch up with her. She was several hundred feet above les Houches, the first village out of Chamonix, and enjoying the trek from the valley floor up through the wooded slopes to Bellevue and Mont Blanc.

'What have you got in there?' shouted her friend. 'Cotton wool? I've never seen anybody set off so quickly with such an enormous sack. It can't just be the wing – you need more of it than that!'

'I'm fit,' replied Simone. 'Anyway, why are you hanging back all the time? Are you ashamed to walk beside me?'

'I'm pacing myself,' replied her friend, arriving at her side in a patch of wild rhododendron. 'We should have taken the cable car to get above the tree line. It saves a lot of time.'

'Tough!' said Simone. 'I do it in the way of the old pioneers,'

'Let's see if you're still there at the end of the day,' said her friend. 'Anyway, this is all wrong. We get up at the crack of dawn, to spend all day walking up through the forest to arrive at the hut shattered – where everybody else is fresh because they've had the good sense to take the cable car, on top of which we haven't seen even started the main climb.'

'Don't keep going on about it, please,' pleaded Simone, grabbing her friend around the neck and planting a warm kiss on his lips. 'I've been good to you. Be nice to me. You know it's something I've dreamed about for such a long time. I want it to last forever.'

'It probably will.'

'Look at the bushes. See how warm and red they are with burning love. Tell me again, what it was that made you change your mind and come back to me? It was someone you spoke to – yes?'

'You know what it was,' he said, in a serious voice. 'I needed someone to teach me how to fly.'

'Oh, you,' she moaned, pinching his cheek. 'That's not what you said at the time. Anyway, I've taught you how to fly. You were the worst pupil I've ever had! Now you do something for me. Come on, mignon, petit *Anglais* – say something nice to me. Please?'

'You're a savage,' he whispered.

'Is that the best you can do?' she cried.

'Okay. How's this? I wouldn't be with anyone else for all the women in the world.'

'Does the one who threw you out count? Back in England.'

'That's a difficult one to measure.' Then he smiled at her, and she knew that she was the only one who counted, for Steve.

'You're more precious to me than anything,' he murmured. pulling him towards her and planting a kiss on her lips.

'If only you meant it, Steve.'

'I never meant it more.'

'And you couldn't live without me?'

'Two weeks ago, I was a living corpse.'

'Me too,' she agreed. 'I couldn't go on. Everything was a cover, you know, please believe, mon petit *Anglais*.'

By mid-morning, they'd climbed above the highest pine trees and reached an area of grassland covered with scattered birches, patches of bilberry and Alpine flowers.

'It's farther than I thought,' she admitted, sitting down next to a pool bordered by cups of marsh marigold.

'You've been up in the clouds for too long,' said Steve. 'I told you it was a full day's walk. We'll reach the Gouter hut by evening, but you can forget the rest of your dream.'

'I'm living on love, darling,' she replied, dipping her fingers into the cool water. 'Don't spoil it. We can do anything, if we really want to.'

'We haven't got wings on our feet,' said Steve.

'One day, we will have, if we stick together.'

'There's another way round it,' he suggested. 'The Tete Rousse lies between us and the Gouter. We can spend the night there, get some sleep and set off fresh in the morning. That way, we don't have to rush.'

'And still build an igloo on top of Mont Blanc? Oh darling,' she enthused. 'You're amazing! All my life I've wanted a man who would make decisions for me.'

'Are you kidding?' said Steve.

'It's true! I feel so full and strong with you. Here, have a bilberry. They're big and juicy. Fill your mouth with them, you gorgeous man.'

Blue gentians and harebells sprang up on both sides of the path. Saxifrage, as red as fresh blood, seeped out of the earth. Patches of purple heather grew up in the spaces between the rocks and long trails of enormous ants carried their booty up and down the track. It was truly a lover's nesting place.

Eventually, the vegetation was left behind and a winding path made of slabby stones led them upwards to a small glacier and the site of the Tete Rousse hut. It was steamy and cramped.

'There are no beds left,' he said.

'And after all our efforts.'

'They've all been taken by people who came up by train.'

'Don't mention them to me,' said Simone. 'It doesn't matter – we don't need a bed.'

'Oh, we just sleep off love.'

'Yes, we do – of course we do.'

He made them both a meal. Simone said little, but she watched him throughout, without taking her eyes off him once.

'That was good,' she said, afterwards. 'You made something from nothing.'

'Nothing is all I have to give,' he replied.

'Me, too,' she parried, with a piercing gaze.

'And now, to bed,' said Steve, clearing the pots from the worktop and draining board, so that they could climb up and get a few hours' rest.

'This isn't how I imagined we'd spend our first night on the mountain,' she whispered, glancing at a dozen or so other climbers who were all over stretched out on the floor of the kitchen beneath them. 'It will be much better tomorrow night.'

The next morning was superb. Skies were clear and the ridges of the mountains were etched out on all sides. Gradually the sun rose, blurring the sharp edges and casting blazing shafts of light into the hollow which was the site of the hut.

They recrossed the small Tete Rousse Glacier, reached its left bank and traversed an icy gully, lacquered with falling stones. Then they climbed an easy rib for two thousand feet, reaching the summit of the Aiguille du Gouter before midday, just as long lines of climbers were returning from their overnight ascent of Mont Blanc. The ridge stretched out, broad and reassuring in front of them. The sun was high and the snow was rapidly turning to slush.

'It's hard going,' he said.

'The air's so thin you don't notice it when you're flying.'

'That's because the gliders do all the work. You can hang about all day under one of those wing things.'

'I'll remind you of that, soon enough,' she said.

'No wonder we're getting some odd looks. They think we're mad. We are! Everybody's coming down and we're still on our way up.'

'Who cares what they think? This is the ultimate high!'

'There's my reputation to consider,' he said.

The steep ascent to the Dome du Gouter was interminable. Halfway up they met a party of guides descending with their clients.

'English?' enquired one of the guides, assuming their nationality from past experience. 'You've left it late. The snow's too soft. The slopes are getting dangerous.' Then he recognised Simone through his dark goggles. 'Simone? *C'est toi – impossible!*' he cried, throwing his ice axe by its point into the snow. Then he turned and looked at Steve Carson, just as Steve recognised him as Bruno, one of the guides from the Alpenstock. 'Ah!' he continued. 'So, I was right. It is the *Anglais* – none other than the hero of the Midi himself.'

'We know what we're doing,' said Simone, sharply.

'Of course you do,' replied Bruno. 'I'm sorry to interfere. After all, I'm only a humble guide. I know nothing about mountains. Does Pascal know about your little excursion?'

'He's not my keeper,' Simone rebuked him.

'Of course not,' said Bruno, glancing at Steve. 'But you know how much he adores his little chou-chou.'

'*Merde!*' spat Simone.

'He'd be crashed out to think of her lying at the bottom of a crevasse – with an Englishman.'

'Come on,' said Steve, trying to pull Simone away.

'A while ago three people were lost, not far from here. Their bodies came out of the Bossons Glacier, as dead as ghosts – is that what you propose?'

'I know,' said Simone, striking out up the slope. 'They were the first to be killed – and they were all guides.'

'Don't say I didn't warn you.' said Bruno, as a parting gift.

'Bruno's a dog,' said Simone. 'He likes causing trouble. He didn't get anywhere with me. If I were to be buried in the glacier with you, I'd be prepared to jump in right now,' said Simone, squeezing Steve's hand tightly. 'Try me if you don't believe it. I'd become a ghost. I've thought about it before now! But not with Bruno!'

'Okay, but not with me either,' said Steve. 'I'll give it a rest till I've got to the top of the Blanc. Then I'll decide who's with me.'

'Me too, I'm not saying I'd go with you – I was just kidding you! Don't take it for granted. Okay, he mentioned Pascal, get it into your head – Pascal might be the one I choose!' The slope levelled out, before it began to rise again. The final ridge was broad, then it narrowed to a single track.

'Which way shall we jump?' said Simone, smiling.

'If you went one way, I'd be sure to jump the other.'

'Traitor!' she smiled. The summit of Mont Blanc was deserted. Its satellite peaks lay below them, and the glaciers licked to left and right, mopping up crumbs of rock on the descent to the valleys.

'It's too flat and round to get excited about,' he said.

'It's the edge of the universe to me. This is where we'll build our shelter. Come on, I'm getting cold already.'

It was exhausting work at that altitude. The air was thin and light. He cut and carried the blocks of snow, while Simone trimmed and shaped them. They smiled but rarely spoke. They didn't have to. They were happy. It was fun.

When the igloo was finished, she cut a hole for the doorway and hollowed out the base. Then, they stood together on the highest point of all, watching the dying rays of the sun tinting the summit cupola. It passed right through them, lighting up their faces. Then, night descended quickly onto the whole mountain.

They were sixteen thousand feet closer to heaven. Soon, they were snug and warm.

'I've waited a long time for this moment. Do you think I didn't want to make love with you? Of course I did – but not down there, in the town. Up here, we can be clean and pure, the two highest people in the whole of Europe. We can really belong to each other, and no one can spoil it for us. Here's a surprise,' she said, removing a double sleeping bag from her sack.

'So that's what you've been hiding. I thought it was a huge sack – why all the secrecy?'

'I didn't want you to see too much into it, too soon.'

'And now?'

'Perhaps I've presumed too much,' she said.

Loving Simone was exquisite – in that small refuge, which they'd made with their own hands, at that altitude, in the rarefied atmosphere of the Alps. It was slow and unhurried. It had to be, but it was warm, too, warm enough to peel back the cover and to look at her. She was the most beautiful animal he'd ever seen in his life.

'Do you like what you see?' she asked.

'You're perfect.'

'That's been said of many women.'

'Not by me.'

'No, you're different. That's why I saved myself for you,' she announced.

He wondered what she meant. Perhaps she'd be sorry. He wasn't an accomplished lover. He was awkward and inexperienced. Perhaps, even now, she contrasted his clumsy efforts with the skill and consideration of all the men from her past. He hurt her. The thought of hurting her was more painful to him than she realised.

'I'm sorry. I have no right to love you,' he sighed, finally.

'No right at all, but I do love you, more than I ever thought

57

possible and I'll tell you now – I might even become a ghost with you if it were possible.'

'You love me?' he said, hesitatingly. 'Well, quick let's jump over the cliff and become ghosts!' She laughed.

'Oh yes, my little one – as in a dream. Joined to you, in this way, in body and soul – as only children can know in life – and the dead only in death. All in the space of time.'

'Tell me again,' he said, seconds later.

'I love you. I love you. Now – in this world and the next.'

'I don't get it,' he said. 'I thought I had no right to love you. You've had many people – I'm English – it's not possible for you to love me.'

'Silly boy,' she whispered. 'I never loved anyone in this way. It's not because you're English,' she laughed. 'Every word of it is true.'

She held him close, all through the night. They couldn't survive outside. She knew that. The journey always took place within. She knew that, too. Some women understand the secrets of the universe. Simone was one of them.

8

Breath Out of Her

In the morning he awoke with her arms still around him.

'Do you still love me?' he said as his first words,

'Of course. I never let go of you,' said Simone. 'I watched over you – all through the night.'

'Were you warm?' he asked, raising himself on his arms.

'As if something good was growing in my tummy.'

'Heavens!' he shouted. 'I'm bleeding,' he said, startled by the patch of dried blood between his legs.

'That must be me,' she gasped. 'I knew that would happen one day – does it bother you?'

'Of course not,' he answered, without giving it any further thought. 'It's just a part of you.'

When he broke open the entrance to their igloo, the sun's rays came flooding in from outside. A new batch of climbers was already gathered on the summit.

'Can we book in?' said one.

'Honeymoon Hotel?' said another, spying Simone's face at the doorway.

'Sort of,' said Steve, lacing up his cold boots.

They were sad to abandon their igloo. Then they descended on the steep slopes of Mont Maudit and Mont Blanc du Tacul – lost in a vast landscape of continuous snow and ice. They could look all around – in one direction they could see Switzerland, in another there was Italy and somewhere to the south there was Provence.

'One day I'll take you to the warmth of Provence – do you see it far, far away!' said Simone.

'We've got to get down from here first; the Vallee Blanche is next, then we'll see the broad glacial plateau which leads towards Montenvers and the Vale of Chamonix. It's about three to four hours.

'No, the Midi,' she responded.

'The Midi? That's the cable-car station. I thought you wanted to walk up and down again, like the old pioneers.'

'No, I've done what I wanted. Now, I've another surprise for you,' she told him, setting off with renewed energy – and arriving at the open galleries of the Midi.

The wind was whipping in and out of the passageways drilled into the mountainside. In a small niche in the rocks a young couple was sheltering. He was about eighteen. She was no older. The boy had saved up for weeks to take the girl by cable car from Italy to France.

It was obvious that he was deeply in love. He'd taken off his coat and placed it around the girl's shoulders to protect her from the icy wind.

The girl looked happy and kept gazing into the young man's eyes.

When she saw the two young people, Simone stopped in her tracks, grabbed Steve by the arm and whispered. 'Isn't that beautiful? They are so much in love. Who'd want to spoil it for them?'

Then she noticed Simone in the queue and quickly said, 'Don't I know you from the paragliding competition in Italy last summer? You won! It was brilliant! You have almost the same name as me!'

'The same name – wow! Yes, it was good,' said Simone, who was quite bashful and reluctant to draw attention to herself.

'Amazing!' said Steve, who didn't know either of them. Then he whispered in her ear, 'It's always nice to get a bit of glory on the side lines.'

'Yes, and don't I know you from the Palais des Gaillands? It's the climbing capital of Chamonix,' said Sisto.

Steve nodded with typical reserve.

'That's fantastic – two world-class climbers and flyers in one day. Pleased to meet you, monsieur!' he said. So did his girlfriend, who was delighted to meet the two sporting fanatics.

'In the beginning a day is almost eternity, don't you think?' said Simone, as they managed to talk their way out of it, with a smile and a shake of the hands. 'See you again – one day.'

'Yes, one day soon – we look forward to running into you again,' said the two youngsters.

'It's odd, meeting them – strange that they should know both of us. Now it's the easy bit,' said Steve. 'I'll go and get the tickets if you don't want to walk down.'

'Not likely,' said Simone, pushing past him and opening a small door built into the wall. 'Splendid!' she enthused, struggling with two huge bags. 'They've arrived.'

'Oh, no you don't,' said Steve, realising what Simone had in mind. 'Forget it! I'm not going over the edge in one of those things – not solo – not from up here – not yet!'

'Steve, they are still looking at us, those two who idolise us. Are they still going to think the same if you refuse to jump! Go on they are showing you how to jump – that's odd! They don't look like jumpers ...'

'Who was it who said you could hang about all day in one of these wing things?'

'You were the best pupil I've ever had,' she shouted.

'I thought that was reserved for someone else. You won't catch me like that, the last pupil you ever had!' said Steve.

'I'll be a fraction of a second behind you,' she argued.

'I want to be the best, but I won't be the best if I'm dead,' he argued quietly.

'Well, okay then,' she said, 'but if I fight it alone, I'll be better than you.'

Ten minutes later, he was strapped into his harness on top of the launchpad. He was twelve thousand feet up on the Aiguille du Midi. There was a four-thousand-foot sheer drop below his feet and nothing between him and the ground but a flimsy piece of nylon. Two people waved and shouted their greetings! as they watched them sprint off down the track.

'I'm right behind you,' she said. 'Remember what I said about the flight and the landing – when the wind's right, do it, as I've taught you.'

'It's okay, it's me that's all wrong,' he thought. 'But how much does she really care about me; is it love? Who's really behind it? What would they think of me down at the Alpenstock if I refused?'

'This is what I came for,' he said, starting his sprint down the runway.

He kept looking up to see if the cells of the canopy were beginning to inflate. Then, he lost momentum. He wasn't running fast enough. The whole wing was starting to collapse above his head. He was teetering on the edge of the drop.

The cold air whizzed past him. He gulped it in as though he were breathing his last. He could sense the icy rocks flashing past behind his back. He had a picture of Simone, Pascal and all the others, smiling to themselves as they wrapped his shattered body in the remains of the glider. He'd been tricked. He was preparing himself for impact.

Then, there was a sudden wrench above him. He thought the glider was about to be torn apart and that he'd continue his journey to the bottom of the cliff. But no. He felt himself being held back. He seemed to be walking on air, drifting away from the icy buttresses, swinging into the line of the sun and floating out over the glaciers, with the pine trees and the green meadows welcoming him home to the valley.

Then he was tripping and stumbling, being dragged downwind and pulled forward by the furl of nylon as it overtook him and bundled him into a large rock. When he looked up, there seemed to be no damage. Everything was intact. He was defying gravity and, more than that, he was still alive. A feeling of euphoria began to creep over him.

Then, Simone appeared alongside him. He didn't know what to think about her. As he circled in the warm air, she'd shadowed his every move, tapping her temple with a finger, trying to convey to him that he was crazy. But inside, he guessed that she must have known that he wasn't ready for a flight like this.

It was true, he had been her best pupil. Why then had he forgotten everything she'd taught him at the last moment? Then, a sense of guilt came over her. Flying was easy for her. She did everything almost without thinking – and she'd assumed that he would, too, even though he was just a beginner. She felt that nothing in him could be less than perfect.

She'd stressed time and again how important it was not only to take off but also to land upwind. He seemed to be speeding up instead of slowing down. 'Christ! He's dead,' she cried, unbuckling her harness and racing towards him. '*Mon pauvre petit Anglais*. What have I done? Oh, what have I done?'

Quickly, she unravelled the last fold of nylon and found him, unconscious, beneath it. She cradled his head in her arms, stroked his cheek and begged him to forgive her. There was no response. 'Speak to me, *chéri*,' she implored him. 'Speak to me, please, or I'll go back and throw myself over the edge, speak to me, speak to me – please.'

For a minute, or more, there was no reaction. Then his eyes began to open, slowly and falteringly.

'Simone,' he whispered. 'Is it you?'

'Yes, my angel, *c'est moi*. I'm here – all yours.'

'All mine.'

'Yes, my darling.'

'No one else's?'

'No, Steve.'

'Not Marcel's?'

'I hate him.'

'Not Brel's?'

'He's a pig!'

'Not Pasc—?'

'He's a beast! I've told you. I'm yours – all yours – all yours – forever.'

'Oh, Simone,' he sighed, closing his eyes. 'Oh, Simone.'

'Don't stop speaking to me, darling,' she murmured. 'Let me hear your voice again. Please speak to me.'

'Speak to you?' he tore into her, suddenly. 'You nearly bloody killed me!'

'Oh, Steve, you're alive,' she exploded. 'You're alright. Oh darling, you were only pretending – I love you, I love you, I love you!' she declared.

'It's a funny idea of love,' he said. 'On the way down I could have been lying in pieces at the bottom of the Midi.'

'It doesn't matter – you proved yourself – if it had been you, it would have been me, next to you.'

'I must be completely mad.'

'Bravo! *Courageux!*' she said, pulling the nylon over their head. 'Look at the beautiful colours. This is our rainbow. This is our pot of gold. We've been to the heights and come back safely.

We are closer than ever we've been. We've peered over the edge and decided we aren't quite ready.'

'You can say that again!' he told her, wrapping her in his strong arms and squeezing the breath out of her.

9

You Aren't Normal

'Ah. You're back,' said Monsieur Maurice the following morning. 'I was beginning to advertise for someone new. I thought you'd never get down in one piece.'

'Me too; in fact coming down was the hard bit.'

'I suppose she went with you, then?' asked Maurice, inclining his head.

'Of course. You couldn't have been more wrong about her – I've had the time of my life with her.'

'That's strange,' said Maurice.

'Why?'

'Because I've seen Monsieur le gendarme coming out of the doorway over there for the last two nights,' he continued, nodding towards the ground-floor entrance to Simone's flat.

'Was it Brel?'

'Of course, she hasn't been in it for long – but he's been there for two months, at least. He has a smile all over his face.'

'Are you sure?'

'Naturally, you want to watch that one.'

'I'm not frightened of Brel.'

'I don't mean Brel! I mean mademoiselle,' he said. 'I wouldn't put it past her to have come down here in the night and sneaked back up to you again the next morning.'

'Don't be daft – that's impossible, she was with me all night long.' said Steve, half considering the idea.

'She can't be trusted. It's not in her nature.'

'Brel must have been trying to find out if she was at home, that's all.'

'Then why the swagger and the big smile?'

'I don't know, Maurice. But I can tell you she was with me.'

'Something's odd about all this business. Are you working today?'

'I'm going to make up to you for two wonderful nights of love.'

'Pah!' said Maurice. 'She'll be the death of you, that gypsy. She marked you out from the start.'

In the afternoon, Simone was flying above the valley with a new client. Steve could pick out her bright red canopy through his binoculars. He wanted to soar upwards to be next to her, but they'd have to wait until the evening, when they were both free. She'd asked him to give her time to shower and invited him round for supper, at nine.

He tried to look smart for once and resisted climbing over the alleyway between her room and his. This time he'd arrive at her door, like everyone else.

He was shocked to meet Raymond Brel under the lamp at the outside entrance. The policeman looked pleased with himself, as usual.

'What are you doing here?' demanded Steve, the moment he saw him.

'I might ask you the same question, monsieur,' the policeman replied, smugly.

'I'm expected,' said Steve.

'Are you saying that I wasn't?' riposted Brel.

'Is she a friend of yours?'

'A friend? Yes, I think so,' replied the policeman. 'As to how good a friend, you'll have to decide that for yourself. I don't give confidence away.'

'What do you mean?'

'Even Simone is entitled to a degree of loyalty, don't you think?'

'Listen, you slimy little rat,' said Steve, pinning the gendarme into the corner of the porchway.

'Go on, monsieur,' said Brel. 'If you're going to do something, do it now, while you can be seen by the rest of the world.' Steve glanced quickly over his shoulder. Monsieur Maurice was watching from the restaurant, as were a number of his customers. 'I'm just going to give you the chance to back off,' continued Brel. 'If you don't, I'll have you arrested. The choice is yours.' Steve cursed, looked up at the ceiling, and stepped aside. 'Very nice, Monsieur,' said Brel, passing in front of him. 'Perhaps you'll find your answers elsewhere? But if I were you, I'd turn around and go home. Home is where you came from.'

Steve Carson smacked the door post with his clenched fist, entered the building and climbed slowly up the steps to Simone's apartment.

'Darling!' she cried, as she opened the door and saw him standing there. 'I'm not quite ready. I've been all in a rush tonight. Heavens! I've never seen you looking so chic.'

'You did say nine o'clock,' said Steve.

'Yes, but I found myself with an extra client.'

'What do you mean?'

'What do I mean, Steve? You know what I mean. There was

someone else waiting for me,' she added, glancing towards the hills. 'It's all money. I couldn't turn him away.'

'I suppose not,' he said, looking around him and walking towards the window. 'You look hot and flustered.'

'Of course, I feel uncomfortable. I haven't had time to shower yet. What's the matter with you?' she asked. 'You aren't upset with me, are you? I'll only be a minute. Be reasonable, darling. It's only for once. It won't happen again, I promise.'

'I've just seen Brel,' said Steve.

'What does he want?' she grimaced.

'Tell me, Simone. What does he mean to you?'

'Brel? Nothing! He doesn't exist for me.'

'I met him at the bottom of the stairs, just a few moments ago.'

'So! You met him at the bottom of the stairs. Oh, I see,' she continued, beginning to get the gist. 'And you think he was here?'

'Was he?'

'Did he say he was?' Simone laughed.

'He said I could get my answers from someone else.'

'Well. It all fits in perfectly, doesn't it?' she said. 'You arrive and me not being ready. It follows that I must have been entertaining another man – a client – Brel, of course. What do you want me to say? To admit that he was here. To deny it?'

'Tell me the truth.'

'You know the truth.'

'We've been so close,' he told her. 'I can't imagine that you'd throw it all away for a few squalid moments with him.'

'I wouldn't!' she declared. 'How can you believe it – after all our time in the mountains? You must be insane – it's gone to your head! No wonder this woman gave you up... Oooh, I can't go on with this.'

'I want to think the best of you.'

'Then think what we've done – together. Don't you trust me?' she asked. 'Even now.'

'It's everything, at the Alpenstock, the names they gave you, "animal", Pascal – I'm trying to forget it, all the time. But it's difficult to wipe out when I'm constantly reminded of it by people like Brel.'

'Yes, okay, it must be my reputation,' she said. 'The stories – the images. I understand how you must feel,' she added, tightening the knot of her bathrobe. 'It's odd, isn't it, how quickly we move from one feeling to another? You'd better go before we become uncivilised.'

'Aren't you going to reassure me?'

'No, if you need reassurance from me, everything we did on the mountain is meaningless.' He looked awkward and helpless. Don't say another word. 'Let's not spoil it all by making idiots of ourselves.'

It was the middle of August, and the town was bustling with holiday-makers. How quiet it had been in Simone's apartment a few seconds earlier. How full and busy the streets were now, even at that hour. How happy they all appeared, as he wandered aimlessly amongst them, gasping for air.

He could smell smoked sausages and the tang of lemon pancakes all mixed into one. The chill from the river revived his senses and made him shiver. He managed a complete circuit of the Place Balmat, before staggering back to the Bar Nash.

'You look ill,' said Maurice, gripping him by the arm. 'I saw what went on earlier. Brel was hoping that you'd do something violent. Now, maybe you've learnt your lesson.'

'Oh, Maurice,' he gasped, 'I could have sworn it – the trouble is – you want to believe it!'

'You aren't the first to be taken in so easily. You can't change someone like that – not even with decency. It runs too deep for words. Here, take a bottle of red – slug it down! Sleep. Forget her. Re-awaken yourself to the mountains.'

He blotted out the night and the light from across the alleyway. His mind started to sink slowly into oblivion. It was almost peaceful. He could hear a voice calling softly to him from a distance. It was her voice, telling him to reach out and to look for her. Her face appeared, ethereally, in front of his eyes. It was disembodied and connected by a silver thread to something indistinct and far off. He seemed to be floating horizontally beside it, pulling himself along by it. The more he pulled, the greater the length of thread appeared to be. It was infinite. There was no beginning and no ending. There never had been – not for souls like theirs. Theirs was not a human love with all its frailties. It was a divine love – nothing could change it. It was all so clear to him now. He could never separate himself from her, no matter what she did in this world of other people. She was his life. He couldn't live without her.

Steve Carson leapt out of bed. 'What time is it?' he wondered. 'Good god!' He'd slept through most of next day. 'Maurice! Maurice!' he shouted. 'Do you need me?'

'You owe me a full day's work!' Maurice informed him from the bottom of the stairwell. 'I let you carry on sleeping so you could exorcise the devil's daughter.'

'Never mind that,' said Steve, fastening his trousers and throwing on his shoes. 'Do you need me?'

'Is it so important you can't give me a couple of hours?'

'Desperately!'

'I might have guessed – you haven't given in, have you?'

'Thanks, Maurice. Don't watch where I go or you might never speak to me again.'

'Don't even tell me. I know it can't be for the good.'

Steve raced across the Place Balmat, dived through the ground-floor entrance of Simone's apartment block and bounded up the stairs.

'Simone! Simone!' he cried, tapping urgently on the door. There was no reply. There was still no answer two minutes later.

It was dusk. She wasn't at the apartment, but he had a pretty good idea where he might find her. Should he wait? Should he set off in search of search of her? He'd walk around the block for half an hour, come back and, if she still wasn't there, he'd reconsider his actions.

When he arrived at the corner of the Avenue Michelle Croz, he looked left towards the Town Hall. Who should be walking down from the police station, en route for his beat, but Raymond Brel.

Steve's heart began to pound, and he immediately shrank back into a shop doorway. Nothing in the world could have persuaded him to make a friend of someone like Brel but, for some reason, he wanted to follow him and find out what he got up to.

There were enough people about to make it possible without being seen, so he followed the policeman, separating his head from all the others bobbing about on the pavement in front of him. To begin with, it was quite exciting; by the end, it became routine, even for Steve.

Brel's circuit appeared to be coming to an end. All he had to do was go across the Place de Saussure and continue in a straight line back to the police station.

After crossing the bridge over the river, Brel suddenly stopped, turned and scanned the whole square. Then, he took a step sideways, opened a small door leading from the Main Street and entered. It was a door almost obscured by posters. If you didn't know it was there, you would hardly have recognised it as a door at all.

A few seconds later, Steve Carson arrived in front of the same door, opened it and found himself in a long, open-air passageway leading to the rear of the buildings bordering the Place Balmat. Simone Carrier's apartment was housed in one of those same buildings.

Steve crept quietly behind the policemen. When he stopped, he could hear the sound of heavy shoes walking ahead of him and, for a second, he could see the dark uniform of the man he was tracking.

He didn't know that there was a rear entrance to Simone's apartment block. It hadn't occurred to him this was the way by which the policeman had always entered the building. You'd only ever seen him coming out again at the front. So had everyone else.

When he got to the next door and opened it himself, Steve expected to hear the sound of Brel's boots climbing the stairway to Simone's flat. But there was no sound. All he could hear was his own heartbeat and the rasp of someone clearing his throat at the end of the corridor. Steve remained perfectly still, listening for the clump of heavy boots which, he was certain, would soon start to ascend the staircase. There was nothing but silence. Then, a light came on and he was convinced that he was about to be discovered.

Someone was standing in the porchway leading to the Place Balmat. Steve crept quietly along the corridor, just in time to see Raymond Brel adjusting his uniform and smoothing his moustache. He could see the sickly smile which came over Brel's face and the deceitful way in which he glanced towards the Bar Nash to make sure that everyone had noticed his presence. Then he exited into the square.

Steve wanted to catch up with him and confront him, but he immediately decided against it. Instead, a wave of remorse began to flood over him. Simone had been telling him the truth from the start. Brel had never been to her apartment, except on the occasion when Steve Carson had first arrived in the town. But he managed to convince everybody else that he had, just by parading and preening himself at the ground-floor entrance to Simone's flat. What else was untrue about her?

He climbed the stairway, just as he had a day earlier. If she wasn't there, he'd be patient and wait for her to come home if. If she was home...

'Simone, forgive me, forgive me,' he whispered, as the door opened slowly, and her lovely dark head appeared in the entrance.

'I wasn't expecting you,' she said, showing him in. 'I thought we'd come to an end.'

'There is no end now. I realise that now. I knew it as soon as we parted yesterday.'

'Yesterday? Was it only yesterday?' she said. 'It seems much longer. It's strange how time slows down when you're suffering.'

'I'm ashamed of the way I acted towards you. I'm so sorry.'

'I have to expect it,' she said.

'Oh, no, Simone. It was all me. I should have believed in you. Do you remember those children we met a couple of days ago on the Midi – Sisto and the girl? I had a dream, and it was all about them. They came to me, and they were happier than I'd ever seen them – I want to be like them – with you. It's true, it's all true – you have to believe me!'

'Wow! That's fantastic, Steve. I want to be wrapped up with you. I should never have got mixed up with the climbing gang – but the boys who were under-age or a bit soft.'

'Mm! Yes, I was one of the gang – yesterday, but the dream thing made me one of the enlightened ones. The fact is, yesterday's dream sent me switched on to everything! I'm back from insanity.'

'What do you mean? Back from insanity?' she asked, resting her head on his shoulder.

'Well, you called me insane yesterday. The old chap inferred that as well. I thought he was like Brel. I had no proof of it, but you can always believe the worst of somebody when you don't have the proof. All he had to do was to feed me the poison – I found him out.'

'How did you get onto Brel?'

'I was convinced that he'd been here. I followed him, through the back door; he hangs about a bit, then comes out of the entrance – he's twisted!'

'Yes, he is – quite a few are, aren't they?' said Simone, with a smile.

'He's odd, but you don't imagine policemen like that.'

'He's not aware that we know, so don't say anything,' said Simone. 'Just let him carry on with his weird fantasy or he'll come back with something else. Steve, don't let's have another misunderstanding about Brel or anyone else.'

'Never again,' he said. He sighed, tightening his grip on her back and closing in on her lips.

'Tell me,' she said, 'did you only come back to me because you discovered what Brel was doing.'

'No, I'd already decided that it was too painful and that dream or something like it was decisive; it made me come here but you weren't in. I ran through the streets looking for you and then I saw Brel.'

'I went to the old man's.'

'I gathered that.'

'He's always sympathetic towards me.'

'You're lucky to have someone like him to turn to. I've got Maurice, but I always end up feeling worse. It's agony.'

When Steve Carson returned to the Bar Nash at midnight, to do a couple of hours' work, he felt at peace with himself, with Simone and the rest of the world.

'It didn't work out, *hein*?' said Maurice, pleased to receive some assistance.

'You know how it is,' said Steve, glumly.

'Women look nice,' continued Maurice, but they're as smelly as cheese – on the inside.'

'You're right, Maurice, and they know how to plaster it all over everybody else.'

'Bitches! I don't mean to add to your pain, but that bloody policeman has been round tonight – I suppose you know that, you saw him come out of her apartment.'

'Brel?' said Monsieur Maurice, contorting his face.

'He's a con!' said Steve.

'I know how you feel.'

'How do you expect me to feel?'

'Yeh, it's tough, *hein*?' said Maurice.

'You'll never know,' replied Steve. 'I feel, well, kind of… bloody marvellous!' he exploded, grabbing hold of the astonished Frenchman and waltzing him round the floor of the Bar Nash.

'What the… you English!' roared Maurice, spilling a pot of sauce all over the floor. 'Are you a complete lunatic? No wonder you've been banned to an island in the middle of the sea,' he blasted. 'You aren't normal. You aren't fit to be with the rest of us – you bloody sausage!'

That's Not Funny

10

'I'm ready,' shouted Simone, leaning over the narrow alleyway which separated the two lovers. 'You see, I take far less time than you when I want to.'

'When you want to, yes,' said Steve, appearing at his window with a face lathered in shaving foam.

'Good heavens!' exclaimed Simone. 'You must be the only climber who doesn't wear a beard.'

'I want to be recognised. It might not interest you, Simone, but I'm going out with a lady tonight! You can decide whether you fit the bill.'

'A lady! That sounds posh. What chance have I then?'

'You could be in the reckoning, if you try a bit harder.'

When he went downstairs to the bar, Steve Carson knew that Simone would arrive a minute or two after him. She always did. Just as he was about to go out into the square, the door of the downstairs entrance to her apartment opened and out walked

Raymond Brel. He went through his normal routine, squinted in the direction of the Bar Nash and walked smartly away across the Place Balmat.

Monsieur Maurice shook his head and gave a long sigh. Steve Carson smiled to himself.

'You've just missed Brel,' said Steve, as Simone came out through the same doorway moments later.

'He makes me shiver,' she replied.

'You look beautiful, Simone,' he told her.

'As beautiful as the lady you were telling me about?'

'Enough to make me ditch her. Anyway, she hasn't turned up. I guess it will have to be you.'

'Where are you taking me?' she asked.

'I thought we would make an appearance at the Alpenstock.'

'You're joking, aren't you?'

'Not a bit!'

'No!' she cried. 'Not there, I hate it! You know what will happen.'

'We'll face up to it.'

'No, Steve, please. We've moved on since then. I'm different now.'

'That's why we have to do it. If we get through that, we're on our way. Another thing, I'm back on form. Rock climbing – it's my thing – the Blaitiere, the Droite, the Verte – in the last three weeks – all with perfect landings.'

'Yes, you told me, but Pascal – he's a fighter.'

'I need to tell Pascal! Wow! I said his name without blinking – now I'm ready for the Dru.'

'Steve, I don't trust him. He's setting you up. He can't wait to bring you down.'

'As long as it's not in a body bag.'

It was almost mid-August, and a gentle breeze was wafting through the town. It caught the top of Simone's black hair and sent small waves cascading over the back of her shoulders.

'Oh, my angel – if I were a painter, I could make a study of you.'

'It wouldn't take long to complete.'

'I'd look at your face every day for inspiration.'

'There's more to me than that.'

'I know. That's why it would take a lifetime of endeavour. Do you think we could stand each other for a lifetime of information?'

'Never mind a lifetime, let's get through tonight.'

'United we stand,' he whispered, as they approached the Alpenstock and stepped over the threshold of the rowdiest bar in town.

It was the most nerve-wracking entrance Simone Carrier had ever made in her life. She never had to share the stage with anyone else. Now, suddenly, Steve was alongside her.

'The animal!' went up a chorus of rough male voices, as they saw her enter the bar. 'It's the animal!' they repeated, again and again. 'Animal! Animal! Animal!'

Nobody expected to see her arm in arm with the Englishman, least of all Pascal, it seemed, who span round in his chair with a broad, though faltering smile, on his face.

Steve Carson stopped in the middle of the floor, made eye contact with Pascal and beyond to pick off the men with the loudest voices.

Almost at once, his strong presence started to have an influence upon the climbers gathered around him. They all knew about Steve Carson. He was a brilliant performer on rock and ice. They nodded in recognition as he passed them by on the hardest climbs. If he'd been sociable, they'd have loaded up with drinks. Some would have stuck an ice-axe into his back but, front on, nobody had the right to challenge him, except Pascal. Soon, there was complete silence.

Pascal dragged the back of his right hand across his mouth, scratched his unshaven cheek and eased himself to his feet. Everybody waited in anticipation.

'So, *Anglais*,' he said quietly. 'A bit more empire-building, *hein*? Sneak into the valley when our backs are turned, settle in, then steal our women – my woman!'

'What the hell are you on about?' said Steve, beginning to square up.

'Don't be insane, Pascal!' said Simone, jumping between the two men. 'You knew all along—'

'Keep out of this, Simone,' growled Pascal. 'I heard all about your little picnic on Mont Blanc. I thought we understood each other, you and me. I thought you were mine.'

'You're drunk!'

'Everybody did. I was up there, staring death in the face; you danced on my grave, the two of you.'

'You're crazy!' said Simone.

'You did, don't deny it. Okay, you know what we do with... snakes!' he cautioned, playing to the crowd. 'In this valley, we sneak up on them – slowly – and when they aren't expecting it – we embrace them!' he roared, lunging forward and throwing his arms around each of them. '*Ah, je t'ai eu Anglais*! I had you! You too, Simone,' he added. 'She was ready. You should have seen your faces! He was ready for action, *hein*, *Anglais*? Come on, I was just messing about. I don't own anybody, least of all Simone. All the best! Good luck to both of you!'

For a moment the crowd of climbers seemed disappointed. Nobody expected a climbdown, least of all from Pascal. He was the only alpinist who could rival Steve Carson, the only one who had a prior claim on Simone, or so they thought. The trouble with Pascal was, you never really knew when he was clowning about or not, but as they all took their lead from him, they reacted accordingly.

'Phew!' went Steve. 'That was close.'

'Pascal, you frightened me,' whispered Simone.

'*Ah, non*,' grinned Pascal. 'It's your life, Simone. You have the right. Listen! Shut up, everybody! From now on, there'll be no more loose tongues. If Simone fancies the Englishman – ugliness has a certain charm about it – well, okay! Anybody who insults Simone, insults me! This is my place! I decide what goes on here. Understood?'

Pascal was the only one who could have got away with it, apart from, perhaps, Carson himself. Some led and others followed – it was always the case. Nobody said a word.

'Thank you, Pascal,' said Simone.

'It's nothing. Let's talk business,' he continued, turning to Steve and leading him towards his table. 'They tell me you've been getting some climbs in recently.'

'Squats on the tops.'

'And push-ups in the valley, *hein*?' sniggered Pascal. 'No, seriously – I get to hear this and that from people. You've been seen on some good stuff. If Simone can manage without you for a couple of days…?'

'It's not an issue,' said Steve, looking for an agreement from Simone.

'We'll go for the new line on the Dru – agreed?'

'Agreed,' said Steve.

'Have you mastered the flying, yet?'

'He's brilliant!' chipped in Simone.

'That reminds me,' said Pascal, turning his attention to Simone. 'You never thanked me for sending the paragliders to the top of the Midi.'

Simone looked uncomfortable.

'That was my idea,' said Steve, coming to her rescue.

'Your idea.' Pascal was astonished by this revelation.

'That's right. I wanted to put myself to the test!'

'Of course,' said Pascal. 'I ought to have realised.'

'I'm the one who should really have thanked you – *mille fois merci!*'

'Let's hope it goes as well on the Dru – and let's hope we all have paragliders. What do you say, Simone?'

There was a veil of mist hanging over the Arve, the grand river which ran down from the Mer de Glace. It was late and they were both sitting next to the statue of Doctor Paccard and Jaques Balmat. Simone was shivering. He wanted to wrap his arms around her, to project, but he also wanted to punish her for her deceit without it leading to another argument or separation.

'I'm sorry,' she said. 'I should have told you when you asked me up on the Midi. We had such a good time – I didn't want anything to spoil it.'

'Your trickery started long before that,' he replied. 'Even that scene tonight was a put-up job. I bet he knows everything about us.'

'Not from me. I was close to him once, it's true.'

'I see – come on, Simone, it was known by everyone at the Alpenstock.'

'No, you don't see,' she said. 'We were just good friends. There was never anything else between us.'

'No, tell all those guys at the Alpenstock!'

'You don't get it, Steve. Pascal is married to the mountains. He only loves himself. If I see him around, we have a laugh. But I don't trust him. He's mischievous. He didn't like it when you said it was your idea to send the paragliders up to the top of the mountain?'

'I didn't want him to think he knew something I didn't.'

'You can never tell with Pascal,' she said. 'Next time I see him, I'll tell him exactly what I thought of his little stunt tonight. Please, darling, don't let him start making us suffer again.'

'No more unpleasant surprises?' he queried.

'No. I'm going to tell you everything.'

'Do we have that much time?' he smiled. 'I'm joking. Come on, let's take Brel's quick way back to the flat.'

The passageway was dark and sinister.

'I thought I was brave,' said Simone. 'But I wouldn't come down here alone.'

He put his arms around her and kissed her. 'I love the softness of your skin,' he whispered.

'I love your strong arms and the thrill of being crushed by you. Let's do it here, now,' she said.

For a second, he wondered what she meant. Then, he felt the desire surging through his own body too. In a moment, he'd pulled her dress down and released her midriff to the cool night air

His hand glided quickly over her thigh and she opened, warm and moist to his irresistible power.

'God! It's wicked,' she thought. 'I love it! I hate it! I love...'

'Oh, Jesus,' she cried. 'Help me, help me, take me, Steve. Stop! No! There's somebody there,' she gasped, breaking the spell which welded them together.

'Where? You're crazy,' he said, panting into her ear.

'No. Listen. Further along the passageway.'

'If it's Brel, he'll wish he hadn't bothered, tonight.'

Not much farther down the passageway came an explosion of passion similar to their own.

'I love you so much,' said a man's voice, twenty metres along the path.

'That's all right,' thought Steve.

'So do I,' replied a second male voice.

Steve's eyes bulged out of their sockets.

'I know that voice,' whispered Simone.

'Which voice?' said Steve.

'The first one,'

'What about the second?'

'Who cares?'

'Who was it?' asked Steve, as the door to the apartment block opened and the two men disappeared inside.

'Marcel!'

'The waiter from the Bar Nash? No!'

'Yes.'

'Your old boyfriend?' said Steve.

'That's right,' said Simone.

'I didn't know that he...'

'Well, now you do know – you still have a lot to learn, *Anglais*. You're so naive at times.' Steve started to chuckle to himself. 'What's the matter now?' she asked. 'If you feel superior, you shouldn't.'

'I don't,' he replied. 'I thought we were the only ones who knew about this place, apart from Brel.'

'Well? And?'

'It seems that somebody else has discovered the entrance to the back passage!'

'Steve, that's not funny,' said Simone.

I Can't Hear You

11

'What do you think you're doing? Where are you going?' she demanded, pulling him back by the straps of his climbing sack.

'To the station,' he replied.

'We aren't going up to Montenvers by train, if that's what you think.'

'There isn't any other way.'

'You know what I think about trains. It's a pleasant day – we'll walk up. That's how you get fit.'

'Hold on, Simone. We've had this conversation before. We slogged our way up Mont Blanc, but I'm not doing it now, with a full sack. You walk up if you like.'

'What's the matter, *Anglais*? Have you not got the legs for it?'

'Are you trying to nobble me before I even get to the climb? I bet Pascal's not sweating his way up through the forest.'

'I don't care what he's doing. I detest trains. They go in straight lines, no matter what's in front of them.'

'That's the whole idea,' said Steve.

'Put your sack on board if you like, but if you care anything at all about us, spend what's left of our time walking up in the sunshine.'

'You make it sound as if I won't be coming back.'

'Who knows if you'll be coming back.'

'Okay, let's presume that I will be...'

Steve left his sack in the driver's cab. Then they began the long walk up the zig-zag path to Montenvers and to his meeting with Pascal at the foot of the Dru. He thought that it would be a good time to get a few things settled between them – but how did Simone see it?

'I'd like to sort a few things out, in exchange with you. I'll tell you about mine. It will be less dramatic than yours. Not a lot happened when I was a kid. All I can say is that it rained.'

'Oh, there was sun *chez moi*! Maybe I'll tell you a few things, but go on, shock me – don't get too carried away with it.'

'Well, she was feathering her nest with me back in England but fortunately the call of the wild had pulled me back to the mountains and started to haunt me. I tried to introduce her to a life out of doors. She wasn't like you, Simone.'

'Oh, thank you, Steve – that's very nice of you.'

'Well, she was too clean.'

'Thanks! Really ...'

'She was too full of dressing-up – and purpose – to succumb to a rough and meaningless existence in the open air – to me she was becoming second best.'

'Who was becoming first best if she was such a dreaded woman?'

'Well, it seemed reasonable to me I'd want to share a woman with her love of the mountains. She was a woman and she wanted that. No compromise was possible – love was her whole existence – so she said.'

'Isn't that surprising, Steve – imagine a woman thinking like that? You were just the same the other night on Mont Blanc. All lovey-dovey.'

'Was I?' Steve looked at her with a cool kind of face – then burst into laughter as soon as she saw her smile.

'Ooo! You!'

'I told her there was something about all women – you get neither warmth nor compassion and you have none. That bit about women being warm and submissive, that's nonsense. I don't mean you, Simone – you show enough of it, don't you?'

'Oh yes, don't I just. For god's sake, Steve, I don't know whether you're talking rubbish or not! She had a point of view; so do I.'

'Yes, that's when she said, why don't you go to France, you talk about it so much? You won't find them as willing as I am! That's when I said, all right, I will, and that was what I did.'

'I thought there was something about another guy who was in the scene.'

'Oh yeah, that's not as important, that was a side line.'

'Well, come on then – what was it?' said Simone, not backtracking from her lead.

'Oh yeah, there was this bloke, he said he was my best friend. He wasn't my best friend – anyway, she turned her attention to him cos he did everything she told him.'

'The suffering must have been unbearable.'

'No, not really – I packed my bags and cursed myself for my own frailty and ran away to the magnificent Alps. I love the snow and rocks! But come on, it's your turn. Tell me about the things that go on in Chamonix and whatever else crosses your mind.'

'No, you're wrong – unlike you, I was born with the sun shining out my eyes.'

'Out of your what!'

'If you're going to be vulgar,' she said, 'I'll shut up.'

'Just trying to be funny and lighten the load. Say it again, Sam.'

'What are you talking about? Anyway, I'll say it again. You didn't tell me everything about when you were young.'

'There was nothing to tell – till I came to France.

'I was born in Provence. The earth is red. The sky is blue, and the sun nearly always shines, even when the Mistral is blowing down from the Alps. We lived on a farm just above the Plaine Dieu. I could see Mont Ventoux from my bedroom window and the Dentelles de Montmirail just over the next hill. They're as sharp as crocodiles' teeth.'

'Wow, it sounds great. I've heard of the Dentelles. It's a popular place to climb.'

'I wasn't interested then. I grew up in a small town called Vaison-la-Romaine. It stands on both sides of a river. The left bank is full of narrow, twisting streets and courtyards with fountains. The roofs are all made of red tiles and grapes grow up the walls of the houses. We lived high up on the right bank. My father has a vineyard. The slopes of the hills and the plane are covered with them. Little villages stand out on rocky crags. There are peach and apricot trees. Lavender grows wild by the roadside. That's where I started off. It's beautiful.'

'It beats where I come from.'

'You don't have to tell me. Anywhere beats where you come from. I was happy. My childhood was magical. I had real friends in those days.'

'And now.'

'True friends fade away with the memories of childhood. Now, there's nobody.'

'You're so tactful at times, Simone.'

'I'm wrong – there is somebody.'

'Well – who is it then?' said Steve.

'My friend is the curse and love of my life.'

'Maybe there's a better way of putting it. A curse, is too strong.'

'It's no joke,' said Simone.

'Perhaps your friend is the love of your life – I've seen it before!'

'It isn't a he – it's a she! That's all I have to say.'

'Tell me about her,' he said, gently, to coax her it out of her.

'It isn't the time. I've lived with it for too long to let it all spill out in one go. Look out!' she cried, suddenly, dragging him in from the side of the track.

'Simone! Have you gone berserk? It's only the sound of the whistle. There's plenty of time to get clear.'

'There's never enough time. Never! Stand back! Let the man go through.'

The zig-zag path crossed the track at several points and the driver whistled to let walkers know that he was coming. It wasn't enough for Simone. The red coaches came rumbling up the slope and passed them by. Simone looked angry and visibly shaken.

'You don't really have a fear of trains, do you?' he asked her.

'No! Of course not,' she said, coldly.

'Okay, we're safe. Tell me more about the name of your friend – not her name if you don't want to, but what did she do?'

'It doesn't matter.'

'Don't clam up on me again,' said Steve.

'I said it doesn't matter. I've told you enough for today. Tell me about your own crummy little town. How often did you see the sun as a child?'

'You're dead right,' he said. 'It was a crummy little town. I didn't know what the sun was until I came to France.'

'I thought as much. You can't beat France, it's incomparable.'

'I'm not arguing,' he agreed.

'And Mont Blanc is out of this world. Gosh, we were the two highest people in the whole of France.'

'The whole of Europe,' he regaled.

'That's why I love it. It's the starting point for big journeys. When are you taking me up there again?'

'When are we going to finish what we started down in the passageway?'

'Oh no! Steve – not that again. You saw the worst of me then. I'm a different person up here. So should you be.'

'Let's stop for a while. We're early. I don't meet Pascal until the afternoon. We could find a little spot.'

'No, Steve,' she said. 'Your body's here, but your mind is still down in the town, I don't want that kind of loving again.'

'A pity,' he replied. 'Spaces to fill but no one to fill them in.'

The path rose steadily above the town. At lunchtime, they sat on the terrace overlooking the Mer de Glace. Small wisps of cloud obliterated the summit of the Dru.

'You won't kill yourself, will you?' she said. 'Not yet.'

'What would it mean to you if I did?'

'It would mean the end of us.'

'Another climber laid out in the cemetery,' he muttered.

'Don't you believe it,' she said, clutching his hand. 'I've got plans for you.'

'What have you got in mind while I'm away?'

'Hm! Now let me see – fly, that's all I do. How long will it be?'

'Hard to say. The top bit's the hardest – still unclimbed. Are you going to fly past?'

'Don't know. Why, do you want me to stay in my room like a goody-goody? That's what you want, isn't it?'

'Staying in your room doesn't make me any happier.'

'Come on, Steve, that doesn't make you any happier. Shall I book in at a nunnery then for a couple of days?'

'Be good. Wait for me. I'll be back as soon as I can. I don't even feel like doing this anymore,' he said. 'Not if it separates me from you.'

'Don't say that, Steve,' she told him. 'If Pascal sees you've got the slightest doubt, he'll be stronger than you. You know what he's like. And you'd hate me later if you don't do what you'd set your mind on. I'm going now, before we get too morbid, I love you. Remember that. I'm complete with you. Without you, I'm finished.'

For a short time, he held her close. Then he started down the track to the glacier. He thought she'd gone, but when he turned, as lovers often do, she was still standing there, waving from the terrace.

'Monique,' she shouted, suddenly.

'What!' he hollered, trying to make out what she was saying.

'Monique! My friend's called Monique. She's a lovely person – she's going to…'

'I can't hear you,' he cried. It was true. The noisy little train was drowning out her voice. Simone looked at it contemptuously, swore and set off down to the town.

Opened His Eyes Wide 12

Mont Blanc is the highest mountain in the whole range. The Matterhorn's shape is ideal, but the Dru is the most spectacular piece of red granite anywhere in the Alps. The rock is sheer for three thousand feet and the climbs are the most difficult and demanding in the whole massif. It was Steve Carson's and was Pascal's dream – they fought each as *vainqueurs* – for Simone!

Steve Carson crossed the grimy ribs of the Mer de Glace, climbed the crumbling moraine and followed a waterfall cascading from above. Pascal was waiting at the top of the scree, where a wedge of old snow pointed towards the climb.

'I was beginning to wonder,' he said. 'You know we need to be at the top of the gully before nightfall. Love changes everything,' he said as a smack in the face.

'My mind is set on this,' Steve lied. 'Let's get on with it.'

They reached the top of the snow and began the hazardous ascent of the gully. It was iced up in parts. Pascal climbed in front of the Englishman, his crampons biting cleanly into the tongue of ice, slithering away in front of them. Steve's movements were stiff and mechanical.

Suddenly there was a worrying sound from above and a huge fragment of rock came down and embedded itself in the ice, just beside him.

Pascal smiled. 'That one had your name on it,' he said. 'What's the matter – you aren't going well?'

'No, but I'm going.'

'Climb with your head, my friend, or you won't have one to climb with at all. We'll bivouac on the large terrace and make an early start tomorrow.'

It was hard going. The sky got darker, and patches of mist began to swirl up the gully from below.

'Damn this weather!' said Pascal. You can smell it in the wind.'

'What's the matter, my friend!' said Steve, finding his rhythm. 'Aren't you going well.'

Pascal smiled and said, 'You surprise me, you don't strike me as the amorous type.'

'What do you mean?'

'When the guys from the Alpenstock closed in on Simone, you didn't mind.'

'I thought the rest of you could have your fill – then I was there for the juicy bits,' said Steve. He played right into the hands of Pascal. It was a line from him, and he ought to have known better.

'I thought you had more about you than that. A bit of fun, yes, but the juicy bits, it seems to have gone to your head.'

'What makes you think that,' said Steve, knowing that he'd put his foot in it.

'Never mind – we'll come back to it later. Keep moving or we'll not make it to the terrace.'

They spent the night on a broad ledge. Between them and the summit lay hundreds of feet of vertical rock.

'Tell me,' said Steve, once they'd bedded down for the night. 'Why put up another route so close to the Bonatti?'

'Why not? Bonatti's crap! Things have moved on.'

'In his day, he was the best,' said Steve.

'Not anymore. He was a traditionalist like you. We do three big faces in a week – you'd fit into just one of our weeks!'

'Better equipment,' said Steve. 'He soloed this when everyone else used combined tactics.'

'He banged in pitons and swung on ropes. This is ten times harder. But it will be soloed – and soon! I'll see to that.'

Steve was waiting for Pascal to bring up the subject of Simone. He hated himself for having betrayed her to the whole crowd at the Alpenstock. But the Frenchman turned over and went to sleep. Somehow it wasn't going to be the kind of ascent Steve had imagined when they'd first discussed the climb.

The air got cold, and the mist disappeared. Stars began to appear in the night sky, and for a long time, Steve looked down at the town and thought about Simone. What was she doing then?

They were up before dawn. By the time the sun had come onto the face, Pascal had already traversed left on some rock flakes and laybacked up an overhanging cracked, stopping on the most strenuous moves and giving the impression that nothing was beyond him.

Steve struggled up after him. When he arrived at a small ledge, Pascal was grinning, shaking his head and staring into space.

'It's your turn,' he said, passing him some gear.

Steve was on the sharp end of the rope. He couldn't afford to make any mistakes, not even minor ones, with Pascal scrutinising his every move. 'This was the move where the lads turned back,' he told Steve, to give him a shock.

'Go on,' said Pascal. 'Bonatti couldn't have done this. We'll do it in less than no time. If you get a move on.'

Specks of orange granite glistened under his fingertips as he moved gingerly up the steep wall. Space started to open between his legs. As he climbed higher and higher above the belay, his hands began to sweat. The wall bulged out over his head. He was a hundred feet above Pascal. There was no more protection. His last runner was forty feet below him. If he fell, he would plummet into the void. He could feel his strength beginning to give out.

'Where does it go from here?' he shouted, shaking out his fingers.

'Work it out,' replied Pascal, knowing that he'd reached the hardest bit of all.

'*Salaud!*' he thought, pulling desperately over the bulge and scrabbling into a tiny recess. It was the hardest move so far.

'How much longer?' shouted Pascal. 'I'm getting cramp.'

There was a slight hesitation when Pascal followed him over the bulge. It was enough to pull Steve through the bad patch and raise his confidence. From then on, they led alternately, one after the other, on every pitch.

The wall loomed over their heads for hundreds of feet. It was exhilarating pitting their skill and wits against each other, as they climbed upward, by cracks and chimneys, slabs and grooves, until, by late afternoon, they arrived at the small platform where Pascal had abandoned his last attempt.

When they looked down, the exposure was awesome. If they fell from this position, they wouldn't touch anything again until they reached the foot of the face.

'It's not the fall that kills you,' Steve murmured. 'It's the sudden stop.'

Pascal looked at him in a funny way. 'Okay, this is it!' remarked Pascal, gazing up the enormous chimney roof which overhung their heads. It was Steve's lead, but the Frenchman was determined to make it his. Not that Steve was going to make an issue of it. Pascal had the right. It was his climb. Steve was only an interloper.

Pascal clipped the slings onto his harness, while Steve was taking a swig from his water bottle.

'You're dead!' he shouted suddenly, making Carson jump and recoil. 'Not you, my friend,' explained Pascal. 'I mean the climb. I'm pumping myself up for the crux. One more rope's length and we've cracked it. For a second, I thought you were about to go over the edge.'

Steve paid out the rope as the Frenchman inched his way upward into the tight chimney. The roof began to impend over his head, until Pascal's body overhung the whole cliff.

Then the chimney got wider, and Pascal had to force himself upwards with his feet on one side and his back on the other.

'I feel as if I'm just going to plop out of it.'

Pascal edged himself upward and outward, but he didn't have the stretch to bridge the gap and remain in contact with the rock. So, he slid and shuffled his way down to his last resting place. The Frenchman climbed slowly back up to his precarious position under the roof. Then he extended himself beyond it, held on by his feet and one arm, while his fingers swept the rock above for a hold.

His body began to wobble and shake. Then, his feet slipped away from under him, and he was left hanging by one arm. Steve could see him fighting to stay on the rock. But it was useless. Finally, his fingers slowly opened, and he fell into the void, with a savage grunt.

Steve could feel the strain come onto his hands. For a moment, it seemed that the whole belay would be wrenched from the rock – and him with it. Then, Pascal swung back onto the cliff and immediately started to climb up to the belay ledge.

'You try, it's your kind of thing,' explained Pascal. 'I couldn't get up last time. I doubt if anyone can.'

It was enough to summon Steve into action. It would make him a better climber than Pascal if he could do it. He changed places with him and worked his way up into the cleft. Then he began to appreciate how difficult it was to stay in the chimney without parting company with it.

'I can see what you mean,' he said. 'It's hard. There's not much to it.'

'You're all right with Simone, she's seen a lot of action but she's clean.'

It was the last thing Steve wanted to hear. 'I don't want to know,' he said, trying to focus his mind on the next few feet.

'You wouldn't want a dose of anything unpleasant, would you?'

'You're beginning to get to me,' he thought, with unacceptable words following.

'Don't be so touchy, *Anglais*. She's yours now, I've already had my fun. I made it plain to everybody. Some women are for marrying. You can't fall in love with a woman like Simone. She has a line in – you know, gadgets, that kind of thing.'

Steve could hear the words echoing up from below. He wanted to focus on the climb. The more he heard the images, they ran with him to the lip of the roof and beyond. A hidden handhold helped him to make the move over the top and get into a more comfortable position.

'I'm almost there,' he said, ignoring everything else.

'That's it,' shouted Pascal. 'There's no more rope.'

'I'll bring you up here.'

'That's suicidal. You're right on the edge.'

'You're kidding,' said Steve.

'I can't hold you from there. Come down.'

'What the hell are you trying, Pascal?'

'It'll be dark soon. We'll never make it. Come down, or I'll pull you down.'

Steve felt the rope tightening around his harness. There were voices above him, as well as Pascal's from below. How he managed to get back under the overhang he never knew, but somehow, his arms and legs slid down into the chimney and he flopped out again at the bottom.

'You're as mad as those from the Alpenstock,' he raved. 'There was enough rope – you knew it!'

'What are you talking about?' yelled Pascal. 'You lost it in the overhang. I saved you from taking us both over the edge.'

'You had other reasons for what you just did,' said Steve.

'*Tu es fou Anglais*,' roared Pascal, whipping open his sack and pulling out a walkie talkie. '*Allo! Allo! C'est moi*, Pascal. We're stuck under the overhang; send down the bags before it gets too dark.'

'We thought you'd made it; we saw somebody,' said Bruno.

'*Non,* we couldn't make it. We'll have the bags now.' A rope was lowered from above. The bags were swinging in space. 'We've got them,' said Pascal.

'I didn't know you had gliders,' said Steve. 'How do I inflate the canopy on such a narrow ledge.'

'Well, you can try it anyhow you like – surely Simone has shown you how, hasn't she? I'd say it was fifty-fifty. It's a free-fall. Just pull the handle when you get clear of the face. It's a piece of cake!'

'The guys still have a comfortable ledge up there. They can throw a rope down.'

'They don't have one now. They're gonna fly down. We'll all meet at the Alpenstock in half an hour – no seven minutes! It's your problem for not getting us over the ledge. Imagine the headlines – from glory to infamy – in a matter of days! I wonder how Simone will take it if you…'

Steve looked up at the overhanging chimney. Could it be done? Unlikely.

'I wouldn't think of that if I were you,' said Pascal. 'You can't resist the challenge, can you, *hein*? But if you make it – I'll tell Simone how you performed on the Dru and I'll make a real hero of you. But then, you've got to make it down, haven't you?'

Then he was gone. Steve watched his adversary plummeting down the face – the paraglider suddenly unfurled and swept

Pascal out over the glacier and towards the valley. He watched till he was just a speck on the horizon, it, appeared, a tearful reunion with Simone – if at all?

Steve pulled on the harness from the paraglider and snapped it into place. A jumble of thoughts and emotions started to flash through his head. What if Simone and Pascal had been in it from the start? The imagery started to flood back into his mind, and he started to think badly of her again.

The granite whizzed by next to his body. Then he hit a projection of rock. His left arm was knocked over his shoulder and round the back of his head. Then, he started to focus his mind and pulled his right arm, tearing madly at the handle which would release the canopy above him.

The sun's rays went out half-way down the face, while above his umbrella of nylon fluttered to maintain its shape. The glacier looked blue. A dark green mantle of pine trees hemmed in the town. Cold air was sinking into the valley, dragging him down far too quickly for his own good. His left arm was bleeding and practically useless. The canopy was out of control and the ground was coming up fast to meet him.

Steve Carson staggered into the Bar Nash and collapsed on a seat just inside the door, about eleven o'clock that night. 'You've just missed her,' said Maurice, unaware of the Englishman's condition. '*Mon dieu!*' he cried. 'What's happened to you? A fight?'

'Where is she?' said Steve. 'I've got to see her now – before it's all too late!'

'It is too late,' said Maurice. 'She's not here. She's gone.'

'What do you mean – gone!'

'Gone! Gone! You know what that means. Gone, with a man, not half an hour ago – what do you expect?'

'Who was it? Pascal?'

'Who? I don't know. Pascal, Francois, Richard, Michel, Gerard. It's all the same to her. She's gone!'

Blood was dripping onto the floor of the Bar Nash. It was pumping through his heart and spurting out through his gashed arm. Maurice was cutting away his clothes. Suddenly, he felt completely calm and detached. It was as if he were looking in on a situation which didn't concern him. Everything was beginning to slow down. Everything was coming to a stop.

'He gave me a fifty-fifty chance of survival. That's quite a big margin, Maurice.'

'Yeah, it's quite a big margin if you fail too. *Marie Salope!*' hissed Maurice.

Steve opened his eyes wide, stared hard at the owner of the Bar Nash, then closed them again.

13

Sun-Baked Place

'Don't dare get up!' stormed Maurice, setting down a tray of coffee and croissants next to his bed.

'How long have I been here?' he asked, grimacing with pain.

'Not long enough.'

'How long?'

'Just one night.'

'What happened?'

'You arrived like a half-slaughtered bull from the abattoir.'

'You said something to me about Simone – leaving!'

'Do we have to go on about that – I lost half my trade!'

'You said something that she'd gone away with another man – who was it?'

'I'm sick of saying it. I was up to my elbows in your blood last night. You aren't family to me and yet I treat you like a son, while you play all over with me. What's the matter? Are you too proud to take advice?'

'Where is she, Maurice?'

'Ah! Maurice, is it? Trying to make a friend of me now?'

'Well, come on,' said Steve Carson.

'I don't know where she is. I don't care. All I know is she went off with another of her clients – somebody older than she was.'

'Are you sure, Maurice, *sûr et certain*?'

'As sure as my better eyes and silver hair can tell. He was tall and thin – had his arm round her like all the rest – and they drove off together, in a nice little car. Does it make you any happier?'

'Not what I expected. No better and no worse. I'll make it up to you, dear friend.'

'Then stay in bed and listen to what I tell you.'

'I will Maurice,' said Steve. 'I will.'

Half an hour later, he was skulking across the Place Balmat, nursing his wounded arm. He followed the track beside the river and crossed the bridge before arriving at the Place du Mont Blanc.

He didn't really expect an answer to the door but, a few moments later, Mr Bourgogne opened it and stood before him, tall and elegant.

'Ah, Monsieur Steve, I was half expecting you. Come in, come in,' said his host.

'Half expecting me?' said Steve.

'Well, someone said you'd be late… and they were waiting for you on the flying field.'

'They wouldn't have expected me. But where is Simone?' said Steve, awkwardly. 'When there's trouble, she always comes to you.'

'Ah, well, that's natural,' said Monsieur Bourgogne. 'But Steve, there is no trouble. There was panic and a bit of a rush, but no trouble. Well, you know that Simone comes from Provence.

'Of course, but doesn't she use a telephone to keep in touch with family and friends.'

102

'She refuses to use a telephone. It's through me that she keeps in touch. It's old-fashioned, I tell her. Did you see Simone's note on your front door?'

'No, not a thing. It's odd, she doesn't keep in touch with family and friends from childhood.'

'Yes. Monique's husband rang. She was her best friend when they were at school – she's having a baby and they want Simone to be there. I offered to take her. She didn't have time to wait at the field – they thought it would be dark soon and you'd put it off till morning.'

'Yes, I'll bet – and did you take her?'

'As soon as I knew from Simone. She refused to go on the train. So, I took her in my car to Vaison. I can tell you it's quite a long drive. It was the least I could do to help. Are you sure you're all right? You're dripping blood!'

'Yes, it's okay. Where is she now?'

'As soon as I dropped her off, I came back here.'

'Would I be okay there, in your car?'

'I don't see why not. She was very worried about you; she told me that you were climbing the Dru. She said she'd promised to be waiting for you when you got back – she put all that in her card and why she wouldn't be there. I think you've got an understanding, Steve. She'll be back in a few days.'

'A few days?'

'She was anxious – as soon as she could.'

'That's put my mind a little more settled, now that some questions have been answered. Tell me, what else do you know about Monique?'

Monsieur Bourgogne looked Steve in the eye, then dabbed at the floor again. 'About as much as you, I suspect,' he said, finally. 'We never forget our childhood friends, do we?'

'Is there nothing else,' said Steve.

'If there is, I can't tell you,' replied Monsieur Bourgogne. 'But I can take a look at your arm, if you'll let me.'

'Do you mean there is more?' said Steve.

'No, no, that was a slip, I understand how you feel. It seems unfair for someone like me to know her more than you do.'

'Maybe you're just as close as I thought in the beginning. Close enough to put her arm round her when it suits.'

'No, oh no. You've got it all wrong – I'm like a father. It's no more than that. I've made my own mistakes. I've learned a little bit over the years. I still have my own hopes. Listen, when she's ready, Simone will tell you everything. Don't mistake an old man's warmth and friendship for anything else. I've told you before. Trust in Simone. She's rather special, isn't she?'

'You wouldn't give me the address in Provence, I suppose.'

'Yes, I have it,' said Monsieur Bourgogne. 'And before you ask me the next thing, I can't give you her telephone number either. But leave things as they are.' He glanced at the papers on his desk. 'She'll be back in a few days – then you can ask her whatever you like.'

'Do you think you could wrap this thing up,' said Steve, looking at his damaged arm, 'It's a nuisance having to ask someone to change it.'

'Of course,' said Monsieur Bourgogne, who said it was a two-minute job and went off to get the required materials. When he glanced at his watch a second time he was pretty convinced that Steve had stolen it, but didn't say a word.

Unlike Simone, Steve Carson loved railways and wondered why Simone disliked them. He liked doing civilised things, in comfort, while travelling along at great speed. He enjoyed walking through the corridors from one compartment to another and looking out on other people's worlds if only to convince himself that his was the best.

This time he was travelling alone, and he was in a car. The train from Le Fayet somehow rumbled out of the station at the same time. Steve was leaving his beloved mountains, just as it had brought him towards them three months earlier.

Now it was taking him to the sunshine and light. The Alps were replaced by limestone escarpments. Vast deciduous forests carpeted the slopes, stretching their green fingers towards the meadowland and the fertile valleys of the Rhone – they were many miles away.

Simone Carrier had travelled there before him and swept her eyes over the horizon as she recalled it. Mont Ventoux rose up like a great marquee, its dusty canvas pierced by the jagged teeth of the Dentelles. The Plaine Dieu was parched and arid, except where it was irrigated by water from the Rhone. She walked between the rows of vines on her father's farm, recalling events from her childhood.

'This was where I ambushed Monique,' she thought. 'Here I bombarded her with grapes.'

It was enough to bring a smile to her lips. It vanished again, almost immediately. Then, she felt a spot of water on her face. It wasn't rain – she knew that. It was the sprinkler, rotating intermittently and spitting its goodness onto the barren earth.

Not that she'd have been put off, even if it had been rain. She loved the rain. She loved the unexpected storms which ravaged the landscape – even in summer. They burst from the skies, with such ferocity, flooding the fields, gushing through holes in the walls, speeding downhill, filling the hollows, sweeping a wall of mud and water throughout the land; they were all too rare for Simone.

This wasn't her kind of country. Neither was it Monique's. That was why they were first attracted to each other, even as young girls. The yearly trip to the *Colonie de Vacances* couldn't come round quickly enough for them. They were both adventurers. They had to escape the flatlands. They had to get away to the hills!

Then they grew up and went to university. At the end of term, they both trained as *moniteurs* so that they could relive their childhood experiences and pass on the joy of summer camp to other children in their charge.

Monique was the more balanced of the two of them. She was more serious – more willing to listen and to learn. Simone knew it. For herself, she was full of the sun and the power of the elements. She wanted to do, and to live and to play unhindered.

'Remember our last holiday in the Alps, Monique?' she murmured to herself. 'Remember how we raced each other down the path? How I tripped and hurt my leg and you tried to carry me all the way down to the valley on your back? Do you remember washing our feet in the ice-cold glacier water during the fifty-kilometre march? And the journey back on the train – all those boys who kept looking at your long legs and making excuses to touch them? Do you remember that, Monique? Do you remember it all? Oh, I do,' she sobbed, bursting into floods of tears. 'I remember it all. It's burnt into my heart and nothing you can say or do will ever free me from my guilt.'

'Simone!' shouted a voice, from the farmhouse. 'It's Armand on the phone. He says you promised to go over today.'

'I'm coming, *maman*,' replied Simone, mixing her tears with the fountain of water coming from the sprinkler. She ran back, barefoot through the vines, her feet streaked with dirt.

'Oh, Simone,' groaned her mother. 'You looked so pretty. Tonight, it's the party and look at you. We see so little of you as it is. What will your father say? You promised…!'

'Tonight is tonight, *maman*. Now I must go to Monique – I owe her that!'

'Simone,' said her mother. 'Look at me, enough is enough. Don't torture yourself every day. Not every day – it's too much. What's done is done. Monique says the same!'

'Not for me. I can never forget.'

'Some people do, Simone!'

'I can't.'

'Monique has made a new start,' said her mother. 'She has a beautiful new baby and all her life ahead of her. The past is dead. She's happy now.'

'Is she, *maman*? Is she? How do you know that? Would you be happy if…?' Suddenly there was a knock at the front of the farmhouse and her mother stopped in mid-sentence.

'Who's that?'

'Monique's expecting me. I'll be back. I'll dress up again for you later. I won't miss your party. I must go by the side door – *maman*, I'll ring you back.'

She jumped the flower bed and careered along a line of small cypresses. Then she stopped dead in her tracks, next to her borrowed car.

'What are you doing here? I sent you a note telling you I was doing this.' She turned her head to the side to see if her mother was watching.

'I borrowed Mr Bourgogne's car and letters.'

'You mean you stole them. Messrs Bourgogne wouldn't have given them to you. If you'd read my note, you'd know exactly why I was here. I won't be long, *maman*. It's somebody I know from paragliding.'

'If I'd read your note I would have died – because you said you were going – I was coming down tomorrow and I wasn't at peace. It was Pascal who said all that. He was out to kill me – or something like it!'

'Don't be stupid. Okay, he was panicking but – I didn't know – I had my own reasons to come here. For god's sake, Steve, there's nothing secretive about Monsieur Bourgogne and me. He told you himself. I told you when you set off for the Dru, I knew it was coming – you didn't hear me, that's all. But I bet it goes beyond the Dru?'

'I heard lots of things – enough to fill a book,' said Steve.

'What things? Oh, don't tell me – Pascal?'

'Things you used to do – with other people.'

'What things! He's a louse.'

'At ten thousand feet, he tells a graphic story!'

Simone's mother appeared at the side entrance. 'Who is it?'

she shouted. 'Haven't you set off yet? You're going to be late.'

'And you couldn't wait another couple of days for me to arrive back in Chamonix? It's somebody from paragliding.' She disguised it from her mother.

'No! No! I couldn't. I was breaking up inside.'

'So, what do you want me to say? I tried to tell you what Pascal was up to. He's using me to get to you and he's doing a pretty good job of it, too. Did you succeed on the climb?'

'What do you think?'

'Obviously not – but he did! – and you let him, in spite of everything I said.'

'It isn't easy to concentrate on climbing when someone's filling your ears with lurid pictures of the one you love.'

'How stupid you are!' she said. 'Why should I have any sympathy for you? You turn up, unannounced, in my parents' home, with a ridiculous story. I knew you'd be taken in. Haven't you learned anything at all about Pascal?'

'It still doesn't seem to put you off him.'

'What kind of naïve world did you grow up in?' she said. 'Stop feeling sorry for yourself. Life's tough. Sure, you can climb useless lumps of rock, but when it comes to anything like a woman's say-so, you just can't dig it, can you?'

'Maybe that's just too much to take,' he laughed. 'I try to forget what people are saying about you. Remember the last time at the Alpenstock, I thought we'd come through. Then, I have to listen to all Pascal's dirt. Simone, it's—'

'Simone!' shouted to her mother, 'Armand's on the phone again. I daren't tell him you haven't even set off yet.'

'Is Armand another of your men from the past?'

'Get into the car!' she ordered, grabbing his bag and throwing it in the boot. Soon, they were rattling down the hill towards the town. 'How did you find me?' she asked. 'By train and bus?'

'By car.'

'What! Where is it now?'

'Next to your car – near the house. We've got to move it.'

He could see the Plaine Dieu, basking in the bright sunlight, and the Dentelles de Montmirail in the distance. 'I like it here,' he said. 'It's quaint.'

'It's too hot for an Englishman,' she said. 'You'd fry.'

'I'd be attracted to the rocks.'

'Just as I said, you'd burn your rosy cheeks. Don't think I'm happy to be pursued – I'm definitely not happy!'

'I'm not happy myself,' he said. 'Nothing's been solved. You'll be happy in a moment,' he said, 'all your dreams will come true!'

The road twisted up into the foothills. Then it levelled out again. The air was warm. You could smell the aroma of lavender and thyme drifting into the car. He felt envious that she'd grown up in such a sun-baked place. He closed his eyes, but he was restless and tormented inside. Nothing had been solved.

14

I'm More Complete

After half an hour, the car squealed to a halt, and she said, 'We're here – I don't know what I'm going to do with you. Hide in the back. But don't follow me in – and don't get out of the car.'

When he opened his eyes, they were parked in front of a small villa. It had pale pink rendered walls, with orange roof tiles and mahogany shutters. There was a new driveway, space on all sides and there seemed to be nobody about.

Simone entered the villa. 'Monique!' she cried.

'Through here,' replied her friend. 'I thought you were coming.'

'Where's Armand?' asked Simone.

'Gone to his brother's house. They decided to let us have the old cradle, after all. She's beautiful, *hein*?' looking proudly at her new-born baby who was lying in a carry cot next to the bed.

'As beautiful as her mother,' said Simone.

'If you hadn't been here, Simone, I couldn't have done it.'

'Don't be silly.'

'Do you want to hold her?'

'She's asleep – I don't want to disturb her.'

'The nurse says she must be fed regularly. I love feeding her myself but it's more difficult in bed. What a pity you can't do it, too, it's really thrilling. I get such nice feelings. I never thought life could be so wonderful.'

'Oh, Monique,' gasped Simone, rushing to her friend and embracing her, as tears welled up in her eyes. 'If only...'

'Don't, Simone. Please – I'm so happy.'

'I'm so sad, Monique.'

'Then be sad for yourself, if you want to, but not for me. I couldn't wish for anything more. Now, come on, take hold of the child.' Simone picked the baby up. It stirred a little, then settled down again. 'See,' said Monique. 'A perfect baby.'

'A perfect mother!' echoed a man's voice from the corridor outside. '*Bonjour,* Simone! Hey! Look what I've just discovered out in the garden, sitting back in a car.'

A handsome young man entered the bedroom, carrying one end of an old-fashioned cot. On the other end of it was Steve Carson, looking shy and nervous.

'Simone, what have you been hiding away from us?' laughed Monique.

'Not what, but whom?' said Armand. 'An *Anglais,*' he added, 'roasting outside in the car.'

'This is Steve,' said Simone, with embarrassment. 'He's just a friend.'

'Yes, a friend, of course,' said Monique, perceptively. 'Come in, come in. let's take a look at you. *Ah, oui, il est beau, Simone. Un peu sauvage*, but a match for someone,' she said, with a twinkle in her eye. 'Are you staying at Simone's? We have plenty of space. You can stay here, if you like. What do you say, Simone, you never told us. What does he do? Steve, are you a flier, like Simone?'

'After a fashion.'

'I don't believe it. You must be an expert.'

'No, I climb a bit?'

'Ah, an alpinist, that's superb!'

'Do you climb, too?' asked Steve.

'*Ah, non,*' replied Monique, instantly. 'In the old... we haven't as much time as we had.'

'Of course, you've just had a baby,' remarked Steve, endeavouring to make a contribution to the conversation. 'But the mountains are so close. Maybe you could start again soon, it would help to get you back into shape.'

'Ah, yes,' said Monique, glancing quickly at Armand and Simone.

'But first we should get this cot set up,' said Armand. 'Hey! There's blood on the side of this... Steve, are you bleeding?'

'Oh, that's me,' said Steve. 'I'm sorry, I cut my arm. It's opened a bit. It's nothing.'

'Ah, non!' said Armand. 'Let me take a look at it.'

'Armand works at the hospital, Steve,' said Monique. 'He knows what he's doing. Simone, you must be getting tired. Put the little one on the bed for a moment,' she continued. 'Lay her across my...' The two women looked at each other and Monique ran her fingers across the top of Simone's head. 'Sorry,' she whispered.

'I'd better be getting back,' said Simone. 'They're having another party tonight; you're lucky you've just had a baby, Monique. Otherwise, you'd have been roped in, too. You know what mums are like.'

'She's alright, your mother. She needs to see more of you. We all do! You aren't going to leave without saying goodbye to us, are you?'

'Of course not. Tomorrow.'

'You're going so soon? And we've only just met your friend. I hope you enjoy the party, Steve. Why don't you let him stay the night with us? Armand will be able to bandage his arm again.'

'No, we couldn't, Monique. It's too much…'

'Nonsense!' said Armand.

'Besides we've only the one car,' said Simone.

'Yes, but we've got yours at my dad's place – don't cause a fuss, Simone – it's the best offer.'

'*Bien sûr!*' said Armand. 'You'll come here tonight and we'll sort you out in the morning.'

'Don't spoil it for us, Simone, it's fine by me,' said Steve, knowing that nothing better had been arranged by anyone else.

'Good! It's all settled,' smiled Monique. 'I won't come and see you off.' Then, quietly, to Simone, 'They told me not to get out of bed till tomorrow. *A demain ma petite. Embrassez-moi. Au revoir Steve. Enchanté!*'

Simone worked out what she was going to say to her parents. She would not introduce him as a paraglider but as a climber from Chamonix who'd been climbing in the Dentelles. He was returning to the Alps the next day.

On one side of the room was a pipe-smoking Russian philosopher, a deputy from Paris, an American countess, as well as the mayor and other dignitaries. Encouraged by her mother, Simone smiled, said a few words to each guest and moved on to the next.

On the other side of the room were some ordinary people, and Simone's father was one of them. He'd made a lot of money from wine, but her father felt more relaxed amongst the ordinary folk, as did Steve.

'I've seen the looks passing between you and Simone. Tell me, how close are you?' said her father.

Steve didn't know how to respond to the question. He hunched his shoulders and looked vacant.

'Is she settled down with you? I don't mean,' pointing to his groin, 'are you happy with her?' he asked.

Steve still didn't know what to say.

'Don't blame her for everything,' said her father. 'Her mother's a snob – most women are. I'm a simpleton myself. I'd put my hands up a cow's backside if I must, but they won't,' he said, glancing at the posh side of the room. 'Simone looks after me. She was always full of mischief. It can all get out of hand at times. You can help her. She's never been the same since… well… she must have told you.'

'What?'

'Hold on,' he said. 'I'm being summoned into the company of the countess. *Merde alors!*' he whispered, setting off across the room.

When Steve found his way back to the small villa, after midnight, Armand was waiting for him.

'Monique's gone to bed,' he said, dressing Steve's wound. 'She was looking forward to talking to you, but she was tired. Another time, *hein*?'

'Yes, another time,' he replied.

Cicadas were chirping in the garden. Their noise went on all through the night. He slept poorly. He could hear the baby crying. Somebody was moving about. He could hear wheels turning on the bare floor tiles. Then Armand opened the shutters and strong sunlight came streaming in through the windows.

'I'm sorry to get you up so early,' he said. 'I'd better wake Monique. She was up in the night with the baby.'

Steve could hear the baby making noises and he could hear Monique speaking back to her in a gentle and tender voice, but she didn't see anything of either of them until breakfast was over and it was almost time to go.

He thought he could hear a car in the driveway. He wanted to say thank you to his host, so he picked up his bag and set off into the corridor. Then, he heard a noise in the next room. The door was open. Monique was sitting on the bed. She looked up at him at precisely the same moment that he looked down at her. His mouth opened wide, in horror and disbelief.

'I'm sorry,' gasped Monique. 'I thought you were outside in the driveway. I didn't want you to see me like this.'

He wanted to turn away from her, but the more he tried, the more he was forced to carry on staring at her. Both her legs had been amputated above the knee. He wanted to speak but couldn't find the words.

'Come in,' said Monique, while he was still staring back at her, in a state of shock. 'Shut the door.' He did exactly as he was told and waited for something else to be said. 'You look repelled,' she continued. 'I apologise for...'

'Oh, no,' he managed to stutter, 'I should apologise to you.'

'It's not the kind of thing you see every day of the week.'

'It's just that I... nobody told me. You must think that I'm very bad-mannered.'

'I thought that you were going to faint.'

'I mean... especially what I was saying about the mountains yesterday. I didn't mean to be so insensitive.'

'You weren't,' said Monique. 'I'm used to it. People don't normally see this side of me. I suppose I get a bit careless at times. I was just about to put my legs on when you called me. You can help, if you like?'

'I don't want to get in the way.'

'It's quite simple,' she said. 'Pass them to me.' Steve picked up the two plastic legs, with the strings and fittings attached. 'They're more shapely than my own ever were,' she said, manoeuvring them into position.

Steve's gaze was magnetised by the ends of the two stumps. The skin and flesh had been stretched around the bone, pulled together and sewn into a kind of bare ball. It was neat but it was white and lumpy with patches of purple and brown.

'Not bad, *hein*?' said Monique, moving each stump of leg independently from the other, in a scissor shape.

'How did...?'

'An accident,' replied Monique, anticipating his next question, but giving no further details. 'But there are worse things in life. I could have been killed. I used to wish that I had been, but I'm alright now. I've got a wonderful husband – I met Armand while I was going for physiotherapy – and now I've got a beautiful baby. I might not have everything I started off with in life, and that's what counts.'

' Yes it does count,' he agreed, admiringly.

'In fact, I wonder how many legless people have climbed Mont Blanc? Now, that really would be a challenge! I'm sorry, I mean...'

'And no frost to worry about, *hein*?' said Steve, warmly, then a little concerned.

'Listen,' she said, 'I can walk on these stilts. I'm very good, but I'm a bit unsteady. They told me to rest for a few days after having the baby, so I'll see you off in my wheelchair, if you don't mind?'

'That's lovely – not a bit!'

'Slip these trousers over the ends of my legs for me, will you – it's rather awkward to reach down. One more thing, Steve,' she continued, 'promise me you won't say anything to Simone about our little conversation this morning.'

'Of course not.'

'You care for her, don't you?'

'Very much.'

'I thought so. She needs a lot of loving. Things haven't always been easy for her these past few years. She gets very emotional at times. You won't let me down?'

'No, not a bit.'

'You'll be good for each other, Steve – I can tell. Now, let's go outside, before she arrives. Life is amazing!' concluded Monique. 'It builds you up, only to drag you down again. I fought my way back, Steve. Nothing more can happen to me – I know that now. Despite losing my legs, I'm more complete than I've ever been.'

As Desperate as You

15

They passed through wondrous sweet meadowland with white mountains and lines of cliffs, adjacent to the road. Then there came small cottages and green hills beside the roadside. There were trees sticking up amongst a fiery red landscape beckoning them on towards Grenoble. About a moment's throw away, something gradually bethought her, and she said…

'Come with me,' said Simone, 'I want to show you something,'

She led him through the tree-lined streets towards the museum. The Egyptian collection was in a room on the first floor. There were many artefacts and a number of mummies.

'Look! Here's a dancer, just 12 years old. They've even got her shoes. And here are some women with skin as brittle as cinder – their skin was brown with torsos coated in shellac. It's as if these people never lived at all,' she said. 'But they did – and they had feelings just as we have. Where are they now?'

'When did you come here?' he said.

'It was in fifth form, at school – but answer my question,' she replied.

'I don't know. Here, I guess.'

'No! Not here, but there – somewhere else,' she said, raising her eyes to the ceiling. 'They believed in the beyond. They built their pyramids in the formation of the stars. They were always trying to get higher into time and space.'

'Is that why you fly?' he grinned.

'Is that why you climb?'

'I climb with my hands and feet attached to wherever the ground happens to be. If it's tilted up at an angle, that's just the way it is.'

'And space?' she said.

'It's all around. But it's not what you think,' he continued. 'It's black and hostile. This is where it's at – make no mistake about it.'

'The trouble with you is, like most men, you have no soul.'

'Yeah, most climbers have no soul – that's why they climb mountains.'

'Yes, they climb to the top, only to go back down – to the bottom again. I have to go up,' she said, 'because I can't go any higher but if I can – I'll do it one day, you'll see. I feel uneasy.'

He was driving his car and they were winding through the deep gorges. Steve loved it. Each time he saw a piece of rock he imagined he would climb it and thought he would tell her about his love of climbing and why she would like it much more if she did it with him. He would take her with him. Then his mind was changed by something altogether different.

'Aren't you satisfied with my explanations?' said Steve.

'What explanations? Nothing's simple with you, like the visit we've just made.'

'Do you mean *chez Monique*?'

'No! Of course not. When we went to the museum. Everything remains a mystery with you. Even when you're

118

supposed to be unravelling things. You always create as many questions as answers.'

'What's bothering you? I've told you everything there is to tell about Pascal. You're huffing and puffing – well, if it's not about Pascal, who is it then? Okay, you just mentioned Monique. What's eating away at you with her?'

'She's nice. She said she wouldn't speak about it – but I can't help it. There's a lot more – I don't know. Yes, I said that I wouldn't say anything to you, but I can't help it. You know more than you say – a lot more. On the walk up to Montenvers, you said she was the curse of your life.'

'I didn't!' she declared vehemently. 'I said she was the love of my life.'

'You did. Tell me, what's wrong with Simone – there's something that's tearing us apart.'

'If something's tearing us apart, it's you and your paranoid behaviour.'

'We aren't getting anywhere,' he said, stopping the car at a picnic area. 'We never do, we never will. It's useless.'

He walked over to a bench and sat down dejectedly, his head drooped in front of him.

'Alright, you say you want to know everything,' she said, approaching and standing over him. 'My God! you deserve it – the way you've pushed and tormented me these last few weeks, driving me mad, accusing me, listening to other people's stories about me. We've come to the end – I know that – I said you couldn't take it. Let's see if I'm right. Where shall I begin? By admitting that I'm worse far worse than you ever imagined.'

'That's just talk, Simone.'

'Is it! Why should I defend myself to you? I am as I am. I was made that way – even as a child. I'm a big girl now. I can look after myself. I always have. If I go back home and do what they expect, it's only because I've got a minimal number of feelings. I don't tell them what I am, what I do. I live my life. If paths cross, from time to time, well, okay, but anyone who gets too close to me knows what to expect. If I have men, it's not because I love them. Nice words and phrases mean nothing to me. If they want their victories, they can have them. It's what I deserve. It's all an act with me.'

'With me too,' he said. 'Is it an act?'

'No! But I'll destroy them – and everyone else too. I always have. It's in my nature to play tricks on people and to deceive them. Even when I'm at my most sincere. You can't know me if I'm telling the truth, I don't even know it myself. I tell people what they want to hear. I paint pictures and dreams, only to destroy them again. Oh, yes, I'm rotten to my core. I have no right to love.'

'Everybody has the right,' he said.

'I haven't! I'm wicked and sinful! I lived another life. I must have messed that one up, too, and now I'm doing the same thing here. Don't feel sorry for me. I don't want your sympathy. I'm in the gutter, just as you thought. I can't change myself, even if I wanted to. It's too late for that. I'm not like Monique; she's strong, she's good. She always was.'

'What of it? You've told me nothing clear and substantial.'

'Listen to him – he sounds just like Brel. Substantial? Do you want to know what I did? You said you wanted to know everything – even about Monique? My best friend. It will be with me till the day I die. I'll tell you. She was innocent – a child, when I was full of worldliness. I always teased her and played tricks on her. I thought it was funny. It was all a joke to me, but like everybody who plays tricks on other people, the joke turns sour in the end.'

'What do you mean?'

'We went to the same school. We stayed weekends at each other's house, even though we lived miles apart. She loved the countryside as much as I did. She used to come to the farm and help us with the grape harvest. When we grew up, she was beautiful. She had long legs. She could run and dance. She even loved the Egyptian girls at the museum when we saw them.'

'She's still beautiful.'

'Yes. All the boys fell in love with her. We used to go camping to the hills – then to the mountains. We used to climb. She was athletic and full of energy – but soft and gentle – feminine. Very feminine.'

'Nothing's changed – she's still feminine.'

'Is she? Then listen. We'd been away for two weeks. We were going home on the train – yes, the train. We were in the last carriage. Some boys were flirting with her. She was wearing shorts. The boys kept brushing against her legs. She tolerated it but she didn't encourage them, as I would have done. I suppose I was a bit jealous. Then we arrived at the station. She lived in the next town and always got off the train one stop before. She climbed...'

'Go on, Simone, don't stop now.'

'She climbed down the steps of the carriage. She had a rucksack, but I had her tent. He asked me to pass it down to her. I started fooling around, hanging onto it and taunting her. The train started to move off. She was standing on the platform, with her hands on her hips. I was just about to throw the tent down to her when she tried to grab hold of it and pull it out of my hands. I held on – so did she. She kept running next to the train. Then, I let go. The weight of the tent unbalanced her, and she fell onto the track. She shouted, but it was too late. The wheels ran straight over her legs. I screamed and someone pulled the cord.'

'That must have been awful.'

'It was – then I ran back down the track. Monique was trying to stand up. Imagine, still trying to stand up with no legs. Isn't that ridiculous? All she could do was to pull herself along by her arms. Blood was pouring out of her like a fountain. I was screaming and going berserk. I didn't know what to do. Her legs were a few metres away. I picked them up and carried them over to her, as if I could stick them back on again. It's sick, isn't it? I couldn't do anything to help. I put my hands over the ends, where blood was spurting out, and all she kept saying was, "It didn't hurt a bit, Simone. It didn't hurt a bit." All I wanted to do was stop time and send it all back the other way again. Just like the train – I've wanted it ever since. She was just 15, she's never blamed me – she's never mentioned it. Even you wouldn't have known if I hadn't told you.'

'No, I don't know,' he replied.

'And the other day, when I was there for the birth, it all came back – even worse. Those disgusting stumps she calls her legs, were thrashing about in the air – the midwife kept telling her to push against something. I grabbed hold of the ends, and she thanked me. God! I could have died. Now you know why I'm not fit to be with decent people that's why my life's worth nothing. Nor will yours be if you stay with me. I threw it all away long ago. You should never have got involved with me that first day. You should never have crossed the alleyway.'

'Oh, Simone,' he sighed. 'Come to me. Don't do this to yourself – and to me. If Monique doesn't blame you, how can you go on, inflicting this pain upon yourself and everyone else? Monique is happy, she's fulfilled.'

'How would you know? Has she told you?'

'It's obvious, she's happy – anyone can tell.'

'Oh, really? Have you seen how she walks? Have you?' said Simone.

'She held onto the tent longer than you – sadly, it was her fault!'

'Yes, but I started it – it was my fault – why did I do it? Maybe I did it, so that I could make up for it later.'

'Yes, that's right, when you've gone to a better place, don't count me in on it – there is no better place than the mountains. She has a physical handicap. You have a mental one and yours is infinitely worse. I can live with it – I have up to now!'

'You haven't! You think your life isn't worth living, so you drag yourself down into the gutter to inflict pain upon yourself, because of something you did in the past, but on top of inflicting it on other people – what about me? Do I have to live with it?'

'No, you can go home; I told you this was the end. We're fighting on too many fronts; Monique lives long away over the hills, but I can't forget her. I can forget Pascal, but you can't, he's still around. I am bad. You don't know what might happen – everything he said about me is true.'

'You don't mean it; that's something to say to the gutter press.'

'I do mean it! Even if it weren't, you could never be sure. I told you I didn't know the difference between truth and lies. I told you I didn't trust anybody. I can't be trusted myself. Everything's working against us!'

'Well, consolidate what we've got. I've had enough of all this pain. We'll come back for the rest when we have to. There are still mountains to climb and stars to visit.'

'Don't go all sentimental on me, *Anglais*.'

'I feel better about us, suddenly,' he told her. 'We've got it out in the open at last. I'm going to do great things from now on. You too; there are ideas to work on, projects to complete. We'll do them together – be part of a team.'

'Even after what you've just said – it won't work,' he told Steve. 'It will all come crashing down.'

'No! There'll be peace from now on. We've come through the worst of it, what do you say?'

'I shouldn't let you persuade me, but I suppose I'm as desperate as you,' she said, hugging him. 'I'll give it a try, you really want me to. But don't say I didn't warn you.' It wasn't the first time he'd heard these words. 'How's your arm now?' she continued. 'I've been worried about you, all alone. You never did tell me how you managed to hurt yourself.'

End of the Tunnel

16

'Oh, you're back again,' grumbled Maurice, catching him bounding up the stairs. 'I'm running a business here and you come and go as if you're a carrier pigeon.'

'It's the beginning of September,' he replied. 'The season's past its peak.'

'Maybe to you,' said Maurice.

'You don't need me. They are all going home now. The town's practically deserted.'

'Funnily enough, I don't sleep through the winter. I must eat all year round.' said Maurice.

'Then you'll be pleased. I'm going through the tunnel to Italy.'

'I'm jumping over the moon. If I don't know why, perhaps you'll enlighten me.'

'Because I can load up with things – meat, wine, anything you like. You know how cheap it is over there.'

'You don't have transport.'

'No, Maurice, but you do. I can take the van – and keep you supplied for the rest of the year.'

'Where do you fit in?' said Maurice. 'Your life revolves round you doing acts of kindness for other people. What's in it for you?'

'Nothing, Maurice. You lend me the van. I take a few things over the border – nothing illegal – fill it with goodies, and whammo! You're stocked up for the year.'

'I don't suppose I get to know what's going the other way.'

'Maurice,' said Steve, slapping a hand on his friend's shoulder. 'Believe me, you wouldn't be interested.' It was true.

Now that he'd patched things up with Simone, however temporarily, he started to think about more productive things. He couldn't take any more suffering and was happier to keep everything else at the back of his mind, in the belief that, just as fate had started to look kindlier upon Monique, things would turn around for them, too.

Besides, he'd managed to get Simone to reveal the root of her problem. There was a new openness about her, even on the rest of the journey home, as if she was being unburdened of a great weight.

The question of Pascal was still unresolved, but he wanted to be more optimistic. He wanted to believe in her. He wanted it to go on. He loved her. The thought of being without her was simply unbearable to him, no matter what she told him about herself. She was far too important to his plans to jeopardise it all by going over everything she'd been told about her by Pascal, or was it because he was just as innocent? Simone was beautiful. Beauty was godliness. The possibility of having it disproved to him was just too much to take.

No, he confided everything in her. He would do something spectacular – something that would set the mountaineering world alight with admiration.

'Three in a row,' he said, the night after their arrival.

'Three in a row?'

'Yes. Draw a straight line from Mont Blanc to the Dru – what lies in between?'

'Le Grand Capucin,' she replied, tracing a line on the map with her finger.

'Correct! We'll do the Frêney Pillar – then the Grand Cap, and we'll finish off up the new route on the Dru.'

'Are you kidding me? It's never been done,' she cried. 'It will take you weeks.'

'We'll do all three – starting before dawn – paragliding between summits and flying back down to the town – all in the same day!'

'That's impossible!'

'Nothing's impossible – not now,' he told her.

'I couldn't do anything like that,' she said. 'I'm a flyer, not a mountaineer.'

'I said we'd work as a team – remember? So we will. We'll take some gear through to the Italian side in Maurice's van. I'll get a good look at the climb – maybe do part of it. You can carry some things up with me.'

'It would be much easier if you could get Jean-Pierre to take the parapentes up in a helicopter. He doesn't much like Pascal,' said Simone.

'I don't trust him. News would get round. I don't want anybody to know – least of all you know who.'

'No, Jean-Pierre's all right. He hates Pascal. He's always trying to get free rides up and down from the mountains.'

'If you really think we can trust him, we need a canopy dropped off on each summit. We can also use him to take photos and to verify the attempt – if it all goes smoothly.'

'It sounds exciting – but I'm frightened. It's dangerous!'

'It's my last piece of work – my final canvas.'

'What do you mean? Your final canvas,' she enquired.

'Something different.'

'Something old, something new.'

'What about me?' she asked.

'You can be the old bit. The new bits over the hills. I liked the look of Provence.'

'What! Move in next to my parents – and Monique?'

'Why not? I'm getting too old for this now. I could write poetry and take up painting. We could settle down there.'

'Or you could write your memoirs,' she suggested.'

'Bloody hell!' he smiled. 'And if we really need to climb – there's always the Dentelles. What do you think?'

'I don't know,' she said. 'I like the Alps. I might not be ready to go to the Plaine Dieu – it's too hot in Provence.'

'We'll talk about it later. Don't say anything at present about the climbs. I'd look stupid if it all comes to nothing.'

'Of course not, chéri. You can trust me,' she said. 'I'm your nearest and dearest.'

No one had seen Pascal since he'd flown down from the Dru, ahead of Steve Carson. It turned out that he'd signed in farther up the valley in Argentière, to be close to the regular twelve boys.

He couldn't admit that he'd injured his ankle on landing, just as Steve Carson had wounded his arm on taking off. Then, he appeared at the Alpenstock, presenting his version of events to anybody who would listen.

Steve kept well clear. His last memory of Pascal was of being abandoned by him on a tiny ledge at twelve thousand feet. Besides, if his plan succeeded, Pascal would hear all about it soon enough and it would put an end to the controversy about which of them was the more accomplished Alpinist.

'I've fixed it!' cried Simone the next day, running into the Bar Nash for the first time in her life.

M Maurice walked in after her with a brush and shovel, and looked, disapprovingly, at Steve Carson, who was polishing glasses behind the bar.

'You look hot and dishevelled,' said Steve.

'That's because I ran all the way here to tell you,' she

spluttered, trying to catch her breath. 'He'll do it. He's not got much on. We can have the helicopter anytime we like.'

'How much?'

'We can sort the price out with him later.'

Steve looked at her suspiciously. 'You haven't come to a private arrangement with him, have you?'

'Oh, Steve,' she groaned. 'How could you? I'm doing my best to show how much I care about you?'

'I'm sorry,' he replied. 'You're right. If we pull it off, there should be something in it for all of us. Did you make him promise not to tell?'

'Of course. He won't tell anybody. He'll do anything to spite Pascal.'

'We'll need to take all the gear up. I'll go with him. Then I can get close to the faces and look at the routes. That will be useful.'

'The weather could be a problem. He says if you wait too long, September can be a stormy month.'

'There are storms anytime in the Alps. But he's right: the longer we leave it, the more chance there is of a longer spell of bad weather. We only need a couple of good days.'

'I could do with a couple of good days myself,' said Maurice, listening in from the other end of the bar. 'You've only just got back. Are you planning another excursion already?'

'No, Maurice, absolutely not,' replied Steve, downplaying his conversation with Simone. 'I'm all yours; in fact, I won't even need to go to Italy anymore, we've come to a different arrangement.'

'Ah!' said Maurice. 'The moment I finish sweeping out the van and ringing Luigi – to tell him you'll be coming to pick up his fruit and vegetables – you'll tell him it's all off again!'

'You didn't want me to go to see Luigi. I thought you'd be pleased to have me around.'

'Who are you trying to kid? You're here now, yes, but you'll be off tomorrow. You've changed, *Anglais*. Now, it's everything that you want – and all because of—'

'We could still go,' Steve interrupted Simone, suddenly. 'Another day makes no difference. We could stay the night in Italy, get the things Mr Maurice needs, and come back the day after.'

'I don't know,' said Steve.

'Don't do any favours for me, either of you,' said Maurice.

'For us, Steve,' she whispered, softly, into his ear. 'We need a break – just to ourselves.'

During the next few days, they made their plans. Simone supplied three new parapentes. They tried them out at Planpraz and Steve perfected his take-off and landing. It would be different altogether on the summit of a mountain, with no runway and variable wind strength. All they could do was prepare for the things they knew about.

Then Steve went up in the helicopter with Jean-Pierre. The view was superb. He got a good look at the Frêney Pillar. It was clean and free of snow and ice. They touched down on the summit of Mont Blanc. He smiled to himself when he saw the remains of the igloo in which he'd spent the night with Simone, He concealed a Parapente in the snow not far away from it.

Then they hovered over the Grand Capucin. He was dangled onto the summit, where he hid another parapente in a cavity in the rocks. Finally, they did the same thing on the Dru.

It was taking a lot for granted, to imagine that he'd be able to complete the three climbs and recover each canopy before flying down to the town – all in one day. Now, it was in the lap of the gods.

A little more than a week after the conception of the plan, preparations were complete, and they were on their way to Italy. It was the first time either of them had crossed the border. The weight of the whole Mont Blanc massif pressed down upon their heads. The tunnel was thick with fumes. It seemed to go on and on forever.

'Look!' she shouted, as they were getting closer to the other side. 'It's just as we thought – the light at the end of the tunnel.'

Merry Go Round

17

It was as if they'd been driving down the slender neck of an enormous pale bottle. When they emerged on the Italian side of Mont Blanc, a great splash of sunlight and greenery illuminated the vast bowl lying in front of them. Now it was Monte Bianco which awaited them, and the character of the mountain was completely different from that on the French side.

In Chamonix, the glaciers and snowfields poured down gracefully from the summit plateau towards the town. In Italy they cascaded into the village of Courmayeur. The great buttresses of the mountain looked mean and intimidating, from this angle, even to someone as talented as Steve Carson.

'I'm worried,' said Simone. 'I love you so much that the thought of losing you to a piece of rock and ice makes me want to do something to stop you going up there. Don't go, Steve, I'm begging you.'

'*Greater love hath no woman,*' he smiled. 'But don't talk like that. You're my rock and you'll be with me every step of the way. I feel good. Everything's falling into place.'

They found a little *pensione* just outside the village. There was a balcony with a view over meadowland and gentle hills, rolling away to the south. He wanted to forget the mountains for a period, but he couldn't.

'I can't see them,' he complained, straining his neck backwards to get a glimpse of the great bastion of rock and ice stretching away behind them.

'That's why I chose this room,' replied Simone. 'We only have a day and a night. Is it too much to ask that you spend your time looking at me?'

'I have the rest of my life to look at you,' he said. 'I can't think of a better way of using up the film.'

'If you really mean it, Steve, call it all off now – you know it will end us!'

'Give it a rest, Simone. When I first suggested it, you thought it was a great idea.'

'Not really. We'd just pulled ourselves back from the brink. I'd have said anything to please you at that moment.'

'You should always say exactly what's on your mind.'

'I'm saying it now. What we've got is too precious to put at risk. You don't realise what it's like for me every time you go off into the mountains, alone. It's torture,' she sighed. 'You've no idea.'

'You've got to understand, it is for me, Simone – I'm doing it for me.'

'Mountains don't matter as much as we do,' she implored. 'Nobody really cares whether you live or die, except me. If it came to that, I'd rather die with you than be left alone.'

'Some hopes!' he said. 'They'd gather round you before the last sod had been laid on my grave. And you know who'd be first in line.'

'Stop it, Steve,' she said.

'It's odd,' he continued. 'You think you know somebody. You think the worst of them – then, out of the blue, they do something completely unexpected. What do you make of it?'

'I don't know. You got what you wanted from him.'

The previous evening, he just got out of the helicopter after a long reconnaissance of the mountains. He was tired and longing to see Simone. Then, in the next street, he'd walked right into Pascal. It was a shock. What he said moments later had turned out to be an even bigger shock. It was the final piece in the puzzle.

'I can't tell you how ashamed I am,' Pascal had confessed. 'I've never abandoned a friend before in all my life.'

'That's not what you were telling them down at the Alpenstock,' Steve had replied.

'You know me, Carson – too much pride. It's just the two of us now. I'll tell you the truth. You were the hero, that day up on the Dru. You climbed better than I. You were in control. More than that – I was just jealous. Nobody's got the better of me. I wanted to pay you back. So, I got at you when I thought it would have the most effect – on the overhang. Everything I said about Simone was all lies.'

'Really? Is that the truth?'

'The truth is, I've never been with Simone at all. I know people think I have – especially in a crowded bar – but she wouldn't let me get close to her – nobody could! She's not what she appears that's a blow to the ego, *hein*? Then, you come along, an *Anglais,* and suddenly you're walking round, arm in arm with her. I joked about it, but it hurt inside. I envy you. I'd even try again if you weren't around. Don't worry, I've got other things on my mind. I've had to lay up for a while. Maybe I don't miss climbing as much as I thought. I'm beginning to see things differently. The world's much bigger than the space you find on top of a mountain. I'm moving on. Let's sign a truce – shake hands on it, *hein*? What do you say?'

Steve held out his hand, almost instantly. He was that kind

of person. He'd accepted Pascal's confession because it seemed a quick and a neat way of tidying up all the loose ends. It was only later, when the euphoria had begun to melt away, that he'd given any real consideration to it. But he had too much on his mind, himself, to think it through. He still had.

They walked into the centre of the village. All the shops were closed. The siesta was even longer in Italy than it was in France. Maybe it was hotter on that side of the border.

They picnicked on a wedge of grass next to the road. Simone cut columns of bread from a long loaf and fed him tomatoes and cheese, with olives. He opened a bottle of cheap red wine and they swigged it all down with relish.

He gazed up at the frontier Ridge. There was a roar from above. Cornices were breaking away. Avalanches were sweeping down to the valley. Simone's eyes narrowed to dark slits.

Steve raised his glass. '*We who are about to die salute you*,' toasting the mountain with a broad grin on his face.

'Don't say that,' she admonished him, 'not even in fun.'

'I'm intoxicated; it's because of you.'

'It's because you're English – you can't take the wine.'

Simone was young. Her head was round and lovely. Her hair was black. Her skin was clear. Her eyes were dark and bright – her features sheer perfection. He wanted to grow old with her and live in a faded room – just like the one they occupied. It was a beautiful room with the lustre of wood and the warmth of rich material all around them. There was the smell of ageing and antiquity and it was timeless.

Loving her, in that small room, in the *pensione*, was heavenly. Not a base thought entered either of their heads. It was sweet, gentle and innocent.

'We're right on the edge of the world,' she said. 'It's been a struggle to get to the top. Now it's all downhill.'

'Because it's easier – or because we're falling apart?'

'Because it will never be better than it is now. You are my first and only love. I waited for you. There was never another before you, no matter what you believe of my past – no matter what you think of me now or what you might think of me tomorrow. But I'm tired, my darling. Now, I'm ready for sleep.'

All night long they lay beside each other, lashed to each other's body, spiced to each other's soul. It was a deep and peaceful sleep.

'That's it,' she said, jumping out of bed the next morning. 'Come on. We've slept too long.'

'It's all very sudden, isn't it? Where's the affection gone?' said Steve.

'Perfection won't get you to change your mind about anything. I must be strong. Besides, we've got to fill up the van.'

'There was a wholesaler's a few kilometres down the valley. As soon as they arrived, they asked for Luigi and handed over Maurice's van.'

'He'll clear us out,' said Luigi. 'Where's that boy Sisto!' he shouted. 'Give us a hand.'

'Leave him alone,' said another workman. 'He's not well.'

'Sisto!' shouted Luigi. 'Where is he? What's the matter with that boy?'

'He's in love,' said the workman.

'In love? That's what it is. Well, we have customers to serve – there's work to be done.'

'He's sick,' said the workman,

'Sick? Don't be daft – he's a college boy, brighter than us. Trouble is, his mind is on mountains.'

'It's not that. I can tell him about being sick, poor little bambino,' said Luigi, mockingly. 'He's not supposed to fall in love – where is he?'

'I'm here,' said Sisto, appearing from behind a rack of shelving.

'Ah! That's where you've been hiding. What's all this about falling in love? What's that to do with you kids, *hein*?'

'I'm all right,' muttered Sisto, dragging a hand across his glassy eyes and picking up the list.

'I don't know – falling in love at eighteen – we were fighting kids at his age – yer know…?

'We've seen him somewhere before?' Whispered Simone 'Don't you recognise him?'

'Vaguely,' said Steve. 'Oh! Yes – up on the Midi. They were keen to grab hold of us there – you nearly bloody killed me!'

'I had other things on my mind. But I was wrong,' she said.

Then Sisto saw Steve and came across to him and smiled. 'I loved your mountain climbs,' he said, and continued. 'they were fantastic. Are you doing any more?'

'No,' he said. It was obviously on Simone's mind, but he thought longingly of her. 'I'm giving them all up, going south to be with my loved one – that's where the heartache belongs,' he said, and looked at Simone knowing it was interpretable.

'Really, is that true?' said Sisto.

'Yes, you can work it out for yourself.'

'They were so much in love. I wonder what's gone wrong,' said Simone. She knew it was full of meaning but which way?

When the boy had worked his way through the list and loaded up the trolleys, several items were missing. Fortunately, his mind had moved on to other things.

'I know what he must feel like,' said Simone. 'Love hurts when it all goes wrong. I have a dreadful feeling. Let's not go back to Chamonix.'

'Not go back?'

'No! Let's head south from here – today. For sunshine – for peace.'

'Go south? I know I said it, but… we've also got a van-load of food which doesn't belong to us.'

'Exactly!' she said. 'We're self-contained. We don't even have to come out if we don't want to. We'll sleep and eat in the van.'

'The van belongs to Maurice!'

'He'll get by. We'll pay him back as soon as we get established. Don't let me down again, Steve – please, it's important. We may never get another chance, please.'

'You're getting emotional, Simone. Life's good for us now. We've come through. We're going downhill to the sun. Remember?'

She looked coldly at him through black eyes – then gave up on the attempt to persuade him.

'On the journey home, there was a helicopter circling around the southern flanks of Mont Blanc.'

'That's where I flew with Jean-Pierre, the other day,' he told her. 'I wonder who it is? I wonder what he's up to?'

They arrived home in the late afternoon. Maurice rushed out of the Bar Nash to greet them. 'Splendid!' he enthused, flinging open the rear doors of the van. 'It was a good idea. You set me up for the year. And you, with such a small brain in your head. Name your price!'

'A couple of days off,' replied Steve.

'Agreed!' said Maurice, carrying in a huge container of cooking oil. 'Well, at least help me. By the way,' he continued, out of the range of Simone, 'someone was asking for you earlier. I told him you'd gone through the tunnel to Italy. Was I wrong?'

'Who was it?'

'I don't know him. He was wearing a red flying suit.'

'Jean-Pierre. What did he want?'

'He wouldn't tell me – so I didn't give anything away.'

'Nothing else?' enquired Steve.

'He asked when you'd be back. I said maybe never. You were returning with a loaded van. There are regulations. It could have been customs for all I knew.'

'Simone!' shouted Steve. 'I've got to go somewhere for a few minutes. Help Maurice carrying in the things, will you?' Simone and Maurice looked most uncomfortable. 'I love you,' he whispered, sprinting across the square.

Jean-Pierre was just about to land in the small field on the edge of the town when he saw Steve Carson. He turned off the engine of the helicopter and the blades came to a stop.

'What do you want?' he asked roughly.

'I was going to ask you the same thing,' replied Steve.

'You were in Italy the last I heard.'

'I'm back. What did you want!'

'They told me you'd gone for good. They said you wouldn't be coming back.'

'Who told you that?' demanded Steve.

'Pascal and Bruno. They said you'd take off with the girl.'

'That's crazy! We went through the tunnel for a night.'

'I thought they were up to something. When Pascal lays his hand on my shoulder, I'm always suspicious...'

'He was covering.'

'I assumed Pascal was telling the truth. I thought you'd never betray me, *Anglais*.'

'Where is he now?' asked Steve, angrily.

'Up on the Frêney. He told me he was taking over from you. He said you knew all about it. You're in love with the animal. I'm sorry – the girl – and that meant more to you than anything else. He knew all about your plans.'

'Who told him? You?'

'Not me, *Anglais*. I hate the bastard.'

'Who then?'

'Get it from Bruno. He's still in town. I'm taking him up to the top of the Dru tomorrow.'

'You! You're taking him? Who dropped Pascal off? Was it you again?'

'Like I said, I thought you'd ratted on me. What would you do? I've got to eat; there's money to be made from this.'

'I'll be back!' said Steve. 'You can count on it.'

He was enraged. The blood was surging through his body. Who could have betrayed him? If it wasn't Jean-Pierre, who was it?

The Alpenstock was empty, and Bruno was sitting alone at a table when Steve appeared in the entrance.

'Now *Anglais*,' he said, lifting his arms into the air. 'Don't take your vengeance out on me. I'm practically a bystander.'

'Who was it?' demanded the Englishman. 'Tell me, how did you get to know?'

'I'm a friend of Pascal's – okay? But I don't want to get drawn into this,' declared Bruno.

'Maybe not, but you'll tell me all the same,' said Steve, threateningly.

'I don't think so, Anyway, I've got things to do,' he added, starting to get to his feet.

Before he got very far, Steve Carson had wrenched his head backwards over the chair and grabbed his neck in a stranglehold.

'Tell me!' said Carson. 'Tell me what I want to know, or you'll be in no fit state to go to the top of the Dru tomorrow.'

'I thought you were supposed to be cool,' muttered Bruno, through clenched teeth. 'Okay. It's nothing to me. It was all part of a deal.'

'What deal?'

'Between Pascal and another party.'

'What do you mean?'

'He'd deliver one thing, if the other party could deliver another.'

'Go on,' said Steve, increasing the pressure on Bruno's neck.

'The other party wanted Pascal to convince someone else that he hadn't been messing around with her.'

'Had he been messing around with her?'

'It doesn't really matter, does it? The point was, Pascal had other priorities. He couldn't believe his luck when everything turned to gold. Get the picture?'

'Vividly,' said Steve, releasing his grip.

'I didn't realise you had so much passion in you, *Anglais*,' said Bruno, leaning forward in his chair and rubbing his neck. 'Pity you won't be part of the celebrations tomorrow.'

When Steve arrived at the Bar Nash, Monsieur Maurice was standing by the doorway with a look of satisfaction on his face.

'Hey! She's alright, that girl of yours,' declared Maurice. 'She's a good worker too. She didn't stop till the whole van had been cleared. I could use someone like her. I'm glad to admit I was wrong.'

'No, you were right,' replied Steve, climbing the stairs to his room. 'You were right all along.'

He was devastated. For more than an hour, he lay on his bed. His head was thumping. His mind felt battered and dazed. Then he went downstairs to the bar, crossed the square and arrived at the outside entrance to Simone's flat. Raymond Brel was about to go through his routine. Steve looked through him and nudged him aside. The policeman seemed disappointed not to have caused more of a reaction.

When she opened the door, Simone smiled weakly. She knew instinctively what had happened. He entered, walked over to the window and turned on her.

'You couldn't have done worse if you told me everything I'd heard about you was true.' It was a controlled voice. 'Why?'

'I don't know,' she said. 'I've always been like that.'

'You knew how important it was to me. We planned it together. You not only betrayed me, but yourself as well.'

'I told you I was capable of ruining everything. I told you what I was like.'

'But why, Simone, why?' he asked her, his voice trembling with emotion. 'What got into you?'

'I wanted you to think the best of me.'

'I did.'

'No. The suspicions you had about him always came between us. I wanted a clean sheet, so that we could start all over again.

139

I want you to be happy. I wanted us to be like Armand and Monique.'

'Even if it meant telling lies about me.'

'There were no lies,' she told him. 'I wanted him to tell you the truth – that's true. He wouldn't have told you otherwise.'

'What truth? You said it yourself, Simone. You don't know the truth! You can't be trusted. I should have known and yet I believed in you, in spite of everything. And all the time, you were plotting against me, deceiving me – telling him my plans – our plans.'

'It wasn't like that,' she protested.

'It was precisely like that. How did you get away with it? We've been inseparable for weeks. Where was I? How did you find the time to conspire with him against me? Was it here – in this room? While I was up in the mountains with Jean-Pierre?'

'It was in the street – and I didn't plan it,' she said. 'I bumped into him, just as you did. He was telling me all about your climb on the Dru. He said he'd been worried about you. He said you'd struggled to get up the climb.'

'That's not the way it was.'

'He said you'd fallen in the chimney near the top.'

'It's a lie, I climbed the chimney. It's all a catastrophe of lies.'

'I didn't know that. I started to think that if you'd get down from the Dru there be something for us. I asked him to say there had been nothing between us. At the same time I was stuck between you still being alive and Monique having her baby. What was I to do?'

Steve didn't say anything.

'Pascal asked for something in return. He said he'd heard rumours that you were planning something big. It just came tumbling out of me. I didn't know you'd hurt your arm. I thought you'd do it before him. He said he understood how I felt. I wanted to save you. I wanted you to be with me!'

'Do you expect me to believe that?'

'It's the truth!' she said. 'It's the truth! He said that he'd had enough – that he was thinking about giving climbing up himself.'

'So much so that he's up on the Frêney this very minute.'

'No! Oh, no!' she cried. 'That wasn't part of our agreement. I didn't think he'd want to steal it for himself.'

'Of course you did. You can't know someone as intimately as you've known him without picking up something about him. He stole my idea, with your connivance. That's why you were here to get me to go to Italy in the first place – when we no longer needed to – and even keener to get me to stay there – because you knew only too well what Pascal was up to?'

'No, oh no, Steve,' she cried, bursting into tears. 'I swear to you. I was just so happy to be with you – so frightened that everything we'd fought for, for so long, would all come crashing down.'

'Just as it has!' he blasted, striding towards the door. 'There's nothing left. How could I ever trust you again after today? How could I ever live with you, knowing you were prepared to sell me to the whole world – or to the last person you've taken into your head? We've come full circle. We're right back at the point I entered your life. You'll excuse me if I don't bother to get on for a second turn on the merry go round.'

18

Oh Where Are You?

He slept surprisingly well, but the moment he awoke, his mind went back, time and again, to the fact that all his planning had been betrayed by Simone. Then, he began to curse her, unwilling to admit that she still existed, a metre away from his own room.

He packed his sack, still unable to grasp that his plan had been hijacked, along with his helicopter and pilot.

On the way out he exchanged quizzical looks with Maurice. The old man grabbed his arm and held him back. 'Are you coming back?' said the restaurateur.

'Sure,' he replied unconvincingly, as if he knew that he wouldn't be.

'Nothing's worth closing up shop for, son,' he said.

'I know that,' Steve Carson replied, tapping his friend on the top of the head.

At lunchtime he heard the whirring of the blades. Then, the helicopter appeared, scything down the valley from Montenvers.

'What are you doing here?' enquired Jean-Pierre, landing in Chamonix. 'You'll only make it worse. Go home. Get smashed.'

'How far has he got?' said Steve, inquisitively.

'He's fast. You'd think he was on the practice rocks. I've had to come down for fuel.'

'Where is he now?'

'On the Capucin. I've got to get back.'

'Take me up with you,' urged Steve.

'It's too late, I'm committed to him now – flying the tricolore and all that stuff. Why go up there anyway? You know who's responsible? Go back and flush her down the toilet.'

'Take me up – you owe me!'

'Even if I did, you're a full day behind. And tomorrow, there's one hell of a thunderstorm moving in on the whole mountain massif – a real tub of dynamite.'

'I don't care. It's mine. I want it. Besides, if he doesn't make it, I'm your insurance policy – a second string to your bow.'

Jean-Pierre grinned. 'He'll make it alright. I despise Pascal, but he's the best. If he doesn't make it, neither will you.'

'I'm not arguing,' said Steve. 'If he's the best, nothing is lost. If he isn't, I'm money in the bank. Give me a ride.'

'He'll rub your nose in it, but I like the odds. Okay, I'll do it – late afternoon. Don't count on me for anything else.'

'Pictures?'

'*D'accord* – but nothing more. You're on your own, from the moment I put you down on the Frêney Glacier, otherwise I'll get flack. Understood?'

'One more thing,' said Steve. 'Is he using my gear?'

Jean-Pierre smiled. 'He couldn't find any of it. Where did you hide it?'

'Up my... you don't expect me to tell you that.'

'That's what we thought. Don't forget – five o'clock – don't be late!'

143

He bought some emergency rations, repacked his sack and waited all afternoon for the return of the helicopter.

He couldn't explain why he wanted to go ahead with this crazy plan. It was completely futile. Maybe it had something to do with filling in time. The alternative to twiddling his thumbs and dwelling on Simone's treachery was to be out on a climb. Putting himself in the kind of danger she'd done everything to prevent. Maybe there was a perverse kind of pleasure in hoping she'd suffer for it, whether he came back or not. All his actions were still dictated by her.

At five o'clock, Steve was still sitting on his sack in the landing field, waiting for his lift up to the Frêney Pillar. When he'd almost lost hope, Jean-Pierre arrived, an hour later.

'You're late,' said Steve.

'You've always been a nation of losers, that's what they say. Let's see what you're like this time. Pascal's already halfway up the Dru. Got some nice pictures.'

'Get me up to the face – and don't push it.'

They flew directly up to the frontier Ridge and dropped down into the dark shadows on the Italian side of Mont Blanc. Then, the small red helicopter lifted off again immediately for a reunion with Pascal and his countrymen on the summit of the Dru.

Steve Carson turned on his headlight and ascended slowly to the plateau at the head of the Frêney Glacier. He crossed the creaking bergschrund and cramponned over the upper snow slope. Towards the foot of the pillar there was a patch of yellow snow – a sign that Pascal had passed that way a day earlier.

It was after ten o'clock. If everything had gone to plan on the other side of the mountain, Pascal would already be celebrating his success.

The night was clear. The air was penetratingly cold and complete darkness enveloped the mighty buttresses rising above his head. Then the moon came up, as he knew it would.

It cast a pale blue tint on the snow and gave him just a glimmer of light by which to climb the easier mixed ground of rock and ice.

He came to a stop beneath a line of cracks, wrapping his arms inside his down jacket, trying to keep warm. It was useless. The cold sapped his body and numbed his limbs until, by degrees, the light from the moon pulled away over the ridge and a new pinkish glow began to trickle in at the edges of the glaciers. It was time to start.

The first hesitant moves took him up cracks and grooves. It was followed by easy rock and a huge corner. There were two more bands of snow.

All morning he climbed, fearlessly, in bright sunshine. Then, he arrived at the base of the great Chandelle. His thoughts turned to those who had died during early attempts on the pillar – now it was laced with pitons, wooden wedges and nylon slings. Here there was no thought of purity. Getting to the top was all that mattered. He pulled on everything, jamming and struggling his way through an overhanging chimney, traversing to the right and reaching the foot of an even mightier chimney, capped by a large roof.

Here, the first doubts began to enter his head, as he hung perilously over the abyss. There were no real handholds. The sun was beating down. His fingers were sweaty. He could find no grip for his boots. His sack kept getting caught up in the chimney.

Wouldn't it be more comforting to float away into the deep chasm lying beneath his feet? There was nothing else for him. Simone had colluded against him with one of her own. Pascal had beaten him at his own game. He'd always believed that he'd come here to die. That had been his mission from the very start. Urged on the edge of the abyss, sweating, drained of all strength, it was much easier to succumb to gravity.

Then, a couple of lines of poetry appeared in his head and he kept repeating them to himself, over and over again: '*For what is there in all the world for me, but what I know and see and what remains of all I see and know if I let go?*'

A savage 'No!' boomed and reverberated around the southern flanks of Mont Blanc and Steve Carson pulled himself over the top, just as the little red helicopter clattered into view. Then, he found himself scrambling over slabs and jamming up cracks again, full of renewed energy. The summit ridge lay in front of him – and finally, the deserted summit itself.

It was just after eleven o'clock in the morning and the sun was beating down on the whole massif. Steve removed his crampons, threw down his axe and scanned the horizon. Great, jagged peaks stuck out, floating on a bed of wispy cloud. The air was thin, but it was pure. What was life at all, if it wasn't this?

He crammed some chocolate and raisins into his mouth, washed it down with a handful of snow and started to look for the paraglider he'd concealed next to the disintegrating igloo.

It was still there, nestling beneath the snow. He felt almost elated. Everything was going well. The wind was coming from the north. He could take off into it and be right on course for his descent to the Grand Capucin.

He opened out the canopy, neatly, on the flat snow behind him, strapped himself into the harness and slung his rucksack over his shoulder. Then, he made his pre-flight checks, just as he'd been taught by Simone. Everything was fine for take-off.

All the peaks below Mont Blanc were glistening in the noonday sunshine. A fresh breeze was blowing over the summit from Mont Maudit. He pulled on the risers and the cells of the glider started to inflate behind him. He could see the canopy filling out above his head. Then, an unexpected gust of wind wafted over the summit, pulling him off balance. The canopy drifted behind him and suddenly he was being dragged backwards over the crest of the mountain.

'Crampons!' he roared. 'No bloody crampons!' He'd removed them and tied them to the lid of his sack. It was a fatal error, and he knew it. His boots gave him no grip on the surface of the snow. He was slipping and sliding towards certain death. In a few more seconds, he'd be whipped over the top of the mountain and sent plummeting 3000 feet to the foot of the pillar he'd just managed to conquer.

Just as he'd given up hope, his back was dashed into something solid. In that split second Steve Carson realised that he'd come up against the half-broken walls of the igloo. In an instant he collapsed the glider, wrapping its lines around the circular structure which had come to his aid. It was a godsend. Simone betrayed him, but her igloo had decided, at the very last moment, to preserve his life. What a paradox!

He removed his crampons from the top of the sack and strapped them, once more, to his boots. A few minutes later, he was flying over the Col de la Brenva and dropping down into the group of pinnacles rising steeply from the Géant Glacier.

It was exhilarating, soaring above like an eagle, losing some height and turning in tighter circles until he could land almost next to the red pillar of granite, which was his next objective.

The east face of the Grand Capucin was in shade. The climbing was intricate and bold, taking a line up vertical walls and threading its way through roofs and overhangs for fifteen hundred feet.

He looked up; he could see other climbers stapled to the rock at intervals. But he wasted no time in tackling the cracks and corners rising above. He felt strong. It was a delight, bridging out in the airy surroundings, traversing first right, then left, apologising to startled climbers who saw him creeping up on them and overtaking them – unable to believe their eyes that here was someone who felt confident enough to solo one of the most difficult routes in the whole of the Alps.

He hand jammed the cracks, laybacked the flakes and

corners, tiptoed up smooth walls, always moving from traction to support, barely on the edge of balance.

All afternoon he climbed, higher and higher, pulling on pitons, clipping the overhangs and reaching back for slings he would need closer to the top of the column. Four hours later, he was standing on the summit, digging out his second parapente, preparing for his next flight, over to the base of the Dru.

He couldn't afford any of the mistakes he'd made on his last launch. The Grand Capucin was an isolated pinnacle with space on all sides. If you got the take-off wrong, there was only one direction in which you could go – downwards.

This time, it went perfectly. The canopy inflated gently over his head and all he had to do was to step into space. 'Two down – one to go,' he thought, drifting over the Géant Glacier, following its broad ribs and turning, in a smooth arc, towards its junction with the Mer de Glace.

Then, he began to wonder what had happened to the helicopter during his ascent of the Grand Capucin. He hadn't seen it since late morning. Who would verify that he'd completed the second climb? Did it really matter? People only wanted to know who'd come first. On the other hand, if, by some twist of fate, Pascal hadn't made managed to…?

As he got closer and closer to his next landing site, he realised that something was happening at the foot of the Dru. He could make out small groups of people in bright clothing, staring up at the face – under one side, on a patch of level ground, was a small red helicopter.

Steve Carson landed, with a whoosh, next to the cluster of people concentrating their gaze on the steep walls of the Dru. Nobody paid him the least attention. They were all too involved in what was happening above. He quickly removed his harness and walked over to the helicopter. Jean-Pierre was on the radio, talking to somebody down in the town.

'Hey, *Anglais* – stay put!' he said, seeing that Steve was about to turn away. 'That insurance policy we talked about. I've dropped the other glider – on top of the Dru. What about the dosh?'

'Yeah?'

'I'm about to cash it in. I got some good shots of you on the Frêney. Did you do the Capucin?'

'Where were you?'

'Where do you think? Bringing this lot up,' he said, gesturing to the group of climbers who were gathered around the base of the Dru. 'I don't suppose I've told you the whole story.'

'What happened?' said Steve.

'He skyed it on the overhang.'

'Are we talking about Pascal?'

'Who do you think? You must have a streak of gold running through you, *Anglais*. By the way, can you prove you did the Grand Capucin?'

'There were plenty of others on the face.'

'Good! Listen, I've got work here, but I'll catch up with you at the top of the pillar – if you make it that far.'

Steve frowned. 'Nobody wants a fall.'

'I thought he was superman!' said Jean-Pierre. 'Remember, I hated him – it's the end for him,' he said, drawing a finger across his throat. 'He was too big for his boots.'

'Has he chopped it?' asked Steve Carson.

'He might just as well have.'

'What do you mean?'

'Ask Bruno – he's the man who saved him.'

'Who, Bruno!'

'I couldn't get close enough and he couldn't move a limb. They need me. The storm's coming in! *A bientôt!*'

Steve knew that if he were to complete all three ascents within twenty-four hours, he would have to start climbing again – and quickly. It was already after four. On the other hand, he was curious to know what had happened to Pascal.

The stretcher was being lowered on a thin steel cable from

the top of the pillar. Bruno was strapped to the side, guiding it down between the rocks. A minute later, it arrived at the bottom of the gully.

'He who laughs last?' said Bruno, spying the Englishman walking across to him. 'I heard you hadn't given up the chase. You've had a bit of luck.'

'What happened?'

'Ask him yourself,' said Bruno. 'He's still alive – and conscious.'

Steve followed the stretcher over to the helicopter and knelt down next to the guide. 'Okay?' he nodded.

Pascal turned his head and looked at him. 'I was right. Bonatti's crap!' he replied.

'How's that?' he answered.

'I lassoed the top of the overhang, just like Bonatti. Couldn't make the pull over. Bombed it over the edge and fell badly on the rope.'

'You'll be back,' said Steve.

'Nothing surer!' said Pascal. 'Hey, *Anglais*. Remember what I told you about the animal? I haven't got it in me to make you feel any better. Think the worst of her – I would. You'll never find out from me,' he smirked. 'See you on the rock.'

'He won't see you anywhere up here again,' said Bruno, whispering into Steve's ear. 'He's finished. He's paralysed from the neck down. I reckon it's the end.'

A chill shiver went up Steve's spine. If a climber couldn't go into the mountains and climb, he might just as well have been dead. For himself, there was no sentiment now; he was re vitalised.

As he walked towards the start, Brel appeared from among the group of rescuers, standing around at the bottom of the face.

'Ah, monsieur,' he smirked, 'I have something to confess to you.'

Steve swore, elbowed him over the edge of the terrace without a word and watched as the obnoxious gendarme spluttered and cartwheeled down the snow slope into a pool of glacier water. He was still smiling to himself as he entered the bed of the gully.

He could hear rocks ricocheting from wall to wall as they were released from above by the melting snow. Any one of them could have cracked his skull open or picked him off and sent him plunging to his death. But he knew he was invincible. He'd come through too much to fall at the final hurdle. The gods were with him, just as they'd set their sights, equally, against Pascal.

In little more than an hour, he was on the wall proper, hand-traversing leftwards. The rock was worn. The friction was good. Each placement of his hands and feet felt solid and secure. It would have been impossible for him to fall. Even if he'd wanted to, something would have closed in on him and pressed his back again, onto the rocks.

Then, there was the rumble of thunder directly above him. If the rock turned wet, climbing in his soft-soled slippers would become treacherous – like motor-racing in slicks. It was the difference between success and failure. He was getting too cocky. Perhaps the gods had had a change of heart?

For the moment, the sun still shone. The rock remained dry, but the noises grew louder. Someone was beating the drum high above his head. Then, he heard the din of the helicopter hovering alongside him, and he was filled with a new burst of energy. His nerve held and he climbed onward again. Up shallow grooves and depressions, up thin cracks and holdless walls.

Then, he arrived beneath the overhang where Pascal had fallen and broken his back. He recalled how they stood together under the same roof a few weeks earlier and how Pascal had taunted him and abandoned him on the ledge, leaving him to fly down alone. He stroked his wounded arm, wondering why he'd paid no attention to it before and why, suddenly, it had begun to ache all over again.

Minutes later, he was stuck into the guts of the roof, battling to stay on. Sucking and leaching at the smooth granite. Then, both feet slipped off the rock and he dangled free, over two thousand feet of space. Where was the hidden hold? Jesus! His strength was just oozing away.

A great clap of Thunder burst immediately above him. The flash of lightning struck the rock and his fingers tightened, instinctively, around the elusive hold. Then, he found himself in the upper chimney, struggling up the final few feet, still bridging out on the suspect rock, as the first heavy drops of rain fell from a black and thunderous sky.

He'd done it! Against all the odds. All that remained was to find his parapente – surprisingly, within twenty feet of his guess – strap himself into the harness and glide back down to the town. Fame awaited him. He'd proved he was the best. Now, he had everything to live for.

Dark clouds were forming all around him. They started to close in, cutting down his view of the valley. He'd never flown in a storm before. Simone had warned him against it. 'Storms and flying don't mix,' she'd told him. 'Don't fly in them, unless you're looking for an early death.'

The air was warm and humid. It was rising and tumbling over the valley. He had to take off in the direction of the turbulence, because that was also where the wind was coming from. But he also had to keep below the cloud or there was the danger of being sucked up into it.

It was difficult to control the lines of the glider. The air was gusting. The canopy kept twisting and flapping in the wind but, this time, he was firmly wedged with his back to the rock. When he ran forward over the edge, the updraft of warm air carried him clear, and he drifted out over the void.

The heavens started to open up. Rain pelted into him. Thunder boomed out over his head. Lightning flashed and battered the mighty pillar of the Dru. Then, he pulled gently on the front risers and the glider went into a shallow drive. All he had to do was keep below the mass of swirling cloud, crackling and foaming over his head. In a couple of minutes, he'd be out of danger and floating back down to the town.

Oh, the town at last! How he knew this was his last climb; he'd beaten Pascal on what he'd come to regard as the best climbing of his career. Now it was time to go down to the sun, to the *soleil*. Oh yes! He could be the big man in town, but was it better to fly right past the flyers' field and go into hibernation?

Jean-Pierre would be waiting for what he called his insurance. Bruno would be there, too, to rub his nose in it. But he'd failed with Simone, and she'd shown him how to love. He loved her and that was the best place to be. How he hated her, but how he was lost without her! Simone, Simone, Simone. Where are you. Oh! Where are you?

19

Soleil

He was right: he'd won the battle over Pascal, but he hadn't won her. Was she waiting for Pascal to be brought down to love him as the wounded warrior and to play the injured woman for as long as she could? It didn't make Steve very happy. Had he come to France to climb a mountain and forsake women? Yes, he had. Had he come to France to die three months earlier? Yes, he had. Though he'd loved the mountains, as he'd said so often, he'd loved a woman. The question was – was the woman as beautiful as the mountains and could they make up for her? Yes, they could almost – he'd realised that from the start! That his vantage point could be part of the rugged natural landscape and so could she – Simone, where are you? Oh, where are you, where are you?

He thought about those covered hills and those rocks which had contained him for so many years. He thought about the wind, the rain and the snow which had sustained him, the sun and the soleil which had carried him over the Alps to the hills of anywhere, with their sun-stroked valleys lying in wait. And her voice which somehow came back to him and spoke to him, and he claimed her. So, he knew that he'd given it all up when she said she'd betrayed him. Was he a fool or a climber of distinction!

A woman was everything to him. She was the almost perfect being, in all ways! Perhaps many others had realised it and so many women – as of men!

On the eastern horizon, there was still a gash of red blood seeping out at the edges. In front and below lay the yellow lights of the town. Then, he became aware of another presence bearing down on him from the north. It was looming downwind, glinting in the sunlight, flashing in the storm. They were converging, each of them, one upon the other.

He banked to the right to avoid a collision. The other object turned straight into his path. He spiralled downwards to lose altitude. So did the other. It was closing in on him, circling around, guiding him back into the eye of the storm. Then, she was upon him, tangled up in his webbing, her legs wrapped around him like the pincers of a crab. How he struggled desperately to free himself from her grip. How he battled to regain control of his steering lines and to veer off in the direction of the town – all in vain.

The two of them were twisted around each other then as much as they had been a few days earlier. They were being drawn into the cloud as surely as if it had been their destiny from the very start.

'You betrayed me!' he roared, more venomously than he had when he'd discovered it. 'You cheated me!'

'Yes.'

'I wanted you. You deceived me! You sold me to the filth of the world. I despise you.'

'Don't say it,' she cried. 'I love you! I love you.'

'I hate you!' he retorted, fighting to get his hands round

her throat, as the pent-up energy burst out of him and he endeavoured to throttle her.'

'Kill me! Go on! Kill me!' she screamed as the two gliders were lifted ever higher into the vortex.

'Monster! You tore away at my heart! Why didn't I listen to them? You knew the truth about yourself.'

'I admitted it,' she wailed. 'I warned you.'

'I should have left you the moment I found out. Anyone who damages a friend is bound to destroy a lover.'

'Do you think I don't know it?' sobbed Simone, fixing her lips upon his and staining his cheeks with her tears.

'Let go of me! Leave me – you wanton lecher!' he raged. 'Go back to where you belong, to the pimps of the town!'

'Look at me! Look at me – Steve, look at me – remember the blood that came out from me?'

'That's a lie – girls have blood every month,' he shouted to her.

'Of course, but not me – I pretended through all those long years – and I played the animal – no one had me before you!'

'Nobody's going to believe you,' he said, as the rotating canopies wrapped themselves around their bodies.

'I did it, Steve, I did it for you – you can call me mad if you like. I am mad because I'll cling to you, even more tightly. I never had a man.'

Stinging rain and opposing currents of air battled for supremacy. It got colder – there was less oxygen. The rain turned solid. It bombarded them, as the updraft lifted them higher into the rarefied atmosphere. The hail was as big as Simone's bloated eyeballs. He hated her. He loathed and despised her lies and betrayal.

And yet, in spite of everything, he felt his resolve beginning to falter, as she appealed more and more for his compassion. He felt the remorse setting in, the desire to protect her starting to overwhelm him. Love and hatred were almost the same – he knew it – as much as he spun round and round.

They were held in a strong embrace. It clasped them as firmly as the tangled lines in which they were being dragged inexorably towards death.

It started to get warm. It was comfortable. Lightning was flashing all around them. It was striking them, illuminating the thin veil of material from which they were suspended. He could see the nylon glowing above them. It was orange and yellow, blue and violet. Still, they rose. It was still terrifying. She was staring instantly into his eyes and hanging onto him in fear. She needed him, more than ever. He couldn't hold out to her any longer.

'Oh! God! I love you,' he sighed. 'I love you more than life itself. I always have. I always will.'

'I love you more,' she repeated. 'You're mine now – mine till the end of time and space.'

'I love you, I love you, I love you,' they whispered, endlessly, clinging on to each other, as the warmth turned to heat and the heat turned into fire. Still she clung to his body, her eyes searing into his. He could feel their sodden clothes steaming and turning molten on their bodies.

He watched her beauty starting to burn up before his eyes. He saw her black hair curl, singe and smoulder. He watched it ignite and flare up in front of him. He smelt it in his nostrils. He saw her flawless skin melting and rippling, along with his own. He could smell the stench of his own flesh. Blistering and boiling. He watched her lovely features turning into an inchoate mass of blood and ugliness. He heard the hiss of fluid and the sizzling and fusing together of their grotesque, charred bodies, their unblemished souls.

'Excelsior!' she cried, with her dying breath. 'Excelsior, my love, ever onward, ever higher,' she sighed, as the fire consumed them and delivered them, whole, into the beyond.

It was the start of a beautiful day. The residue of the storm had burnt itself out in the early hours of the morning. Now, the sun was mounting in the sky and the steam was rising from the meadowland, south of Courmayeur. Soon, the ground would be dry again.

Sisto Carucci passed in front of the newsagents on his way to a new rendezvous. He had no time to read the headlines of the morning newspaper. If he'd glanced at the billboard outside, the details hadn't gone in.

'Death and disaster on the Dru.'

Sisto Carucci had other things on his mind. It was a morning of reconciliation. He felt ill. He felt sickly. Would she still want him? Would she even bother to turn up at all?

When he arrived at the end of the lane, she was already waiting for him. He was on time, but he apologised to her as profusely as if he'd been late.

The sky was blue over Monte Bianco. It rose sheer and resplendent over the valley. It reminded him of the glorious day that he'd taken her up there, weeks earlier, in the cable car. That was what had inspired him to go back again without telling her. Now, he'd saved up enough to make a second trip, if she cared to accompany him. She smiled and said it was possible.

The first tentative words exchanged, he felt bold enough to take her hand in his. She looked shy but didn't resist. He led her towards a field. The grass had been newly mown. They sat down side by side on the yellowing hay. It was dry. He coaxed her gently backwards.

'Let's go together,' he told her. 'Whether there be mountains or if the hills don't do it for us, let's get married and cling to each other.'

'I'll cling to you more tightly – I never had a man,' said Simone.

'Yes, we'll have lots of babies!' shouted Steve.

Small creatures were buzzing, flitting and hovering all around them. Sisto could feel them landing on his face and arms. When he opened his eyes, they were everywhere, floating and falling, like petals from out of a clear sky. They landed next to them and on top of them.

When he looked more closely, they weren't flying insects at all, but fragments of material, reflecting in the bright sunlight. They were orange and yellow, violet and blue. They were large and small, regular and ragged. It was strange, he thought – small pieces of nylon, falling in a column from out of the sky, each of them scorched and congealed at the edges.

'Oh, Sisto,' she murmured. 'Hold me – kiss me. Love is everything,' she added.

'Everything!' he agreed, holding a small piece of burnt nylon between his fingers. 'It's as infinite as God, as timeless as the stars – so is your name – Simone. That's funny,' he said. 'I didn't realise – it just came out, I'm sorry.'

'That's okay, my name is also Simone – it's the same as Soleil, like that girl – it's sunshine all the way through to the nice bits! Soleil,' she said.

'Wow! That's not bad at all, is it? No, not bad at all.' They turned to each other and laughed, and laughed, and laughed till all the tears ran down their face! 'Simone Soleil, Simone Soleil. Yes, that's a perfect name; it's absolutely perfect! Simone Soleil!'

This book is printed on paper from sustainable sources managed under the Forest Stewardship Council (FSC) scheme.

It has been printed in the UK to reduce transportation miles and their impact upon the environment.

For every new title that Matador publishes, we plant a tree to offset CO_2, partnering with the More Trees scheme.

For more about how Matador offsets its environmental impact, see www.troubador.co.uk/about/